Your Matches

HEIDI PINE

ISBN: 098875200X
ISBN-13: 978-0-9887520-0-9

DEDICATION

For Marion Marr.

CONTENTS

ACKNOWLEDGMENTS

The biggest acknowledgement is to NaNoWriMo for inspiring people to write. A special thank you to my friends and family, who supported my writing, gave me time alone to write, and listened to me talk endlessly about the characters I created.
This book contains real and fictional establishments in Orange County and Nashville. References are made to multiple online dating services, too.

1 LAWRENCE – SUNDAY NIGHT

It was time to update his online dating profile. What kind of bait would go on the line tonight? Last week it was all about the swimming. That fucking bitch. She had to take the oldest boy up to the swim meet and leave him with the others.

How dare she? He had things to do. Caring for two brats was not part of it. He had done his time. He had done every single thing that he was supposed to do. He coached the kids' soccer teams, baseball teams, and even helped with the girl's ballet. Cub Scouts, check. Boy Scouts, check. Babysitting, no.

That was why he wrote the checks to that bitch. It was her job to take care of them! That was why he went to work. That was why he needed someone to take care of these kids.

One wanted to watch the never-ending World Series of Little League. He was sick of kids' sports, sick of watching the boy obsess over it, and sick of the whining for him to sit down so they could watch it together. He was sick of seeing the kid sit around the house with headphones in and the game on his iPad.

He had told the boy to turn it off and play outside. The kid had to get up and make himself useful. What made that kid think he could just drift through life so entitled he didn't know how to pull weeds, mow a lawn, wash a car, make a sandwich. Fuck, the boy couldn't even dry a dish.

That bitch. She just kept spoiling the kids. They weren't kids anymore. They were robots. They didn't even get their hair cut properly. He couldn't even see their eyes when he looked at them. The brats were reduced to just a flop of hair covering their faces as they asked for money for another damn electronic device that turned them more into zombies and removed

1

them further from the concept of being capable, able-bodied humans.

How could these be his offspring? The older boy, sure. The older boy was good. He got it. The temptation he knew the boy was running into, well that was another story. He knew that teens in the area were smoking pot, having sex, getting drunk, and stealing their parents' exotic cars for joyrides along the coast. It wasn't always in that order, and it didn't matter. It was temptation. If his older boy....

Profile, profile. The lovely Delores would be taking care of the little ones this week while he was at work. Delores fell for what he put out last Sunday. He had known he had to find someone who would adore him and make sure the kids were out of his hair. That meant they had to like her, respect her, and not have a single thing to complain about when he picked them up at 5 o'clock sharp. She had to be unmemorable and enchanting at once. She had to be smart enough not to ask questions, and dumb enough that she couldn't answer any either. This was delicate.

There were so many to weed through, and he had to find just the one. It took two days to get her, and that was all he had. That was a lot of effort as far as he was concerned.

Delores was perfect. She had to be. Fuck, he was good at this. He nailed it.

Profile, profile. What to get this week...

It had to be the sympathy card. Yes, he'd play the sympathy card. He wanted to be treated gently and not have to work hard this week. It would be enough with Delores to pacify and dealing with the two kids after 5 pm. That was just so much work. This week had to be easy. This one had to melt in his gaze. Sympathy it was. He quickly typed in the sympathy script and signed off.

Sometimes it was just too easy. It was a lot easier to get back to the kids now. Everything would fall into place tomorrow. It always did.

2 DELORES – THREE WEEKS AGO

It was sunset, and the fresh summer air was just the right temperature with a light breeze flowing onto her terrace. Delores looked out at the Pacific Ocean from her perch in Newport Coast. Deep bittersweet joy and sadness always came to the surface when she took a moment to be quiet and feel the peace surrounding her. Her effort to enjoy the moment always left her feeling grateful for all that she had, and at the same time like hers was a life that had not bloomed. In these moments, she couldn't help but be increasingly honest with herself. The only great thing she had done was being her daddy's little girl. Her daddy, Juergen, was her world.

Delores had never really known the love of a mother since hers had died in childbirth. Nelda had been the only mother figure she'd had. This efficient servant had been kind and loving in the most detached way. Nelda never uttered a word about her mother. Nobody did. It seemed to Delores as though her mother never had existed.

Growing up, all that existed was her and her daddy and a fun, happy world. Nobody expected anything from her other than a smile. She was usually happy, too, so it was easy to smile. Toys, ponies, other girls to play with, going to fancy cities with Daddy on the jet, and everyone smiling and adoring her.

She always had loved going to Europe, where they would visit castles and ride on narrow roads through snow-covered mountains that looked like a container of vanilla frosting with sugary sparkles sometimes, and like lemon meringue pie just moments later. Sometimes they had gone to the Alps in the summer, and it was like someone had drawn a landscape just for her where she could run through the grass and pick wildflowers, dancing in the sun. She was possibly the happiest girl on earth, and her dimples and

3

freckles with flowing blonde hair made her look like nature's princess.

Her enjoyment and happiness made Juergen smile. It even made his new wife smile. His new wife was not interested in children and did not try to be a mother to Delores. She was always kind, and Delores remembered feeling very special when they would smile at each other. Delores was allowed to be free her entire life.

Today Delores was living in the house Juergen had bought when Rita, his fourth wife, became his fourth widow three years prior. Delores had always been Daddy's little girl, even with the wives and widows. After his mourning periods, Juergen wouldn't dare let on to anyone that he was suffering. However a year after Rita passed, it was clear that Juergen had undergone a drastic change. He was not able to return to his daily routine. He did not smile or communicate and instead faded into a hollow existence in the Newport Coast mansion.

As Juergen withdrew from her and everything else, Delores was terrified. He was her life. She didn't give a second thought to moving out of her Wilshire penthouse and into Daddy's house. He would offer a half-hearted smile at her happiness. It seemed they both knew neither one was happy, and they both knew he no longer had the will or determination to go on.

All the grief suddenly came to the surface and Juergen was consumed with the sadness and loss that he'd buried so industriously for years. His own mortality had become his only reality. Each of the four widows had taken such a piece of her father that each day in the Newport Coast house she could be less and less Daddy's girl. It hurt to see her father suffer. She couldn't help but question if he would have preferred to have her mother around instead of the daughter who must remind him so much of his one true love.

Delores had a sense of guilt for being alive. Her birth had taken the life of his true love and eventually three more women who were his companions after her mother died. Why did she get to live when her mother's life ended so young? She wondered if he ever really loved her, or if it was just the image of her mother that he loved. Did he really want her in his life? Had he ever wanted her in his life? Was he always reflecting on how much her mother would have loved to see her smile? Every day Delores battled to deny this guilt and the questions it evoked.

Throughout the year following Rita's death, Juergen forgot how to care for himself. He became incapable of conversation. Delores would come home from shopping and find him sitting in the middle of the dining room table, just gazing at the seam of the wall and ceiling. He would wander into the kitchen and put his clothing in the cabinets. He became unpredictable except that he only would wear his smoking jacket over burgundy satin pajamas. The pajamas were not clean.

It was crushing to her spirit. Delores faced the most difficult reality of her life when he was diagnosed with Alzheimer's and it was apparent that she was not equipped to care for him. She placed him in a special residence for seniors with dementia and Alzheimer's.

He didn't even know whom she was when she visited. At times Delores was convinced it was her own fault because she no longer recognized herself either. He called her every woman's name with adoration, and it didn't really matter because for all she knew that is who she was inside.

Today, though, something new had happened. While they sat in the large wingback chairs, tea table with the afternoon decaf tea and remnants of the sugar-free cake between them, Juergen had called her by her mother's name. Gertrud. It was the only time she had ever heard him say her mother's name. It was with a love that touched her deep to the soul and had every cell in her body invigorated. Daddy was so happy. In her struggle to remain positive and maintain some routine in her visits to him, she felt like finally it had mattered. If only for a second.

"Oh, Gertrud, wouldn't you just love to have a child? You would be the most extraordinary mother. Nothing on this earth would make me happier than to see you with a child. What do you think? I can see it now, how your belly will change as a little person in there grows ready for this world. Oh, Gertrud, what will it be?"

Beaming, Juergen had reached out and grasped Delores's hand in his own. Delores smiled. Juergen beamed with more radiance than she'd experienced since Rita's passing.

"Yes..." Delores did not know what else to say. "Yes."

She had felt a pang of sadness connecting like that and hoped her eyes did not betray her smile.

The moment was gone in a flash, as Juergen looked at her curiously, "Mrs. Blaire, what ever are you doing here? I just made a deposit this morning and told you I would be in next week. Is something awry with my account? So nice of you to join me. I always have appreciated the personal service you provide."

Again, Delores smiled and responded, "Yes."

She excused herself and returned home to watch the sunset.

Delores was no longer Daddy's girl. Daddy as she knew him was gone. She had to let go. It was up to her to find the way now. She felt like a hologram in her own life. If people could see her, really see her, then they would know she was not real. Delores knew Juergen didn't know she had not been happy for a long time, and for this she was grateful.

Who was she if not Daddy's girl? Now she was an adult in the world he had helped her create. As much as she missed him, no tears came to her eyes as she looked out over the Pacific Ocean. She was her father's daughter.

What beauty.

Her reflection was interrupted by two brief yipping sounds from Ferdi and Polly. The two royal red poodles stopped their constant sniffing of God knows what to greet Nelda, who was carrying out a silver platter with a lovely supper. Ferdi and Polly pranced over to their outdoor dining room and followed their training perfectly as Nelda placed the meals in front of them, adorned them in white bibs, and bowed her head to give thanks to the Lord. The dogs sat upright and with their front paws held up for 15 seconds before they were allowed to eat the natural, organic meal that had been prepared for them. Nelda disappeared into the mansion without a word. She would be back in exactly five minutes to remove the bibs, brush their silky red fur, and take them to their room to retire for the night.

Delores watched as the two dogs ate. Ferdi and Polly were her babies, and Nelda was raising them. She thought again of that brief exchange with her father today and returned her gaze to the Pacific Ocean. The colors were changing to deeper shades of purple and orange, fading over the horizon as she felt her life was.

She was 40 years old. Was it to late to consider being a mother? Her own mother was 41 when Delores was born. Why had she never considered this question?

Darkness set in, and with it absolute solitude.

Monday morning came quickly after a solid night of uninterrupted sleep. Delores approached the wall of windows 20 strides from her enormous California King bed, opened the French doors to the balcony, and inhaled deeply. At 5 am, there was always a lingering of darkness before dawn broke, and this was Delores's favorite part of the day. After five minutes enjoying the delicate salty air, again nursing that bittersweet cocktail of emotions, she went back inside and dressed for her daily ride on her road bike.

Today she planned to ride down the Pacific Coast Highway to the canyon road, and turn toward Santiago Canyon before looping back along the riverbed to the coast. Few cyclists rode alone as frequently as Delores, complaining that it was boring. The solitude was part of the fulfillment she got from the sport, though. She had ridden with biking groups in the past and found the others to be a melting pot of vulgar, common, and boring.

Goodness, she even had dated some of the men from the riding club in Malibu. She had hoped that sharing a common interest would elevate the level to which the relationship may lead. It did nothing of the sort. While it was fun to ride together in new places, escaping to the mountains of Colorado or the endless terrain in the underrated state of Pennsylvania, there was little to discuss off the bikes. Most of the time the sex was pedestrian and unfulfilling, and the men were too lean or obsessed with their training. Why did she have such a knack for meeting these vain princess-like men?

Most of her childhood and college friends had scattered around the globe. They were married with children, and their lives had revolved around diapers, day care, fund-raising events, and schedules that were dictated by the children's activities. In fact, they seemed quite bored. Few had put their education to use as Delores had. Instead they slaved to the demands of their husbands, children, and country club colleagues.

In the spring, her best friend Wendy had come to visit, eager to spend time reminiscing while her husband rewarded their twins with a trip to Brazil in honor of middle school graduation. Of course the topic of Delores's solitude came up. Wendy insisted it was time for her to stop being Daddy's girl and to accept a real man in her life.

Ignoring Delores's hesitation, Wendy created a profile to market her on two dating sites. She said one was only to check the activities of her matches on the other as a measure to ensure they were not playing multiple women on multiple sites. Delores did not understand why the shenanigans were necessary. What kind of game was this anyway? She had not engaged in it. Her time had been too precious in the spring since she had been wrapped up entirely in the fading of Juergen to a man who no longer resembled her father.

As Delores climbed the canyon, she became less resistant to the online match system. Maybe at the very least she could get out for an adult conversation with someone who remembered the name he was calling her from one moment to the next. How long had it been?

It was 8 am when Delores stepped out of her sweaty road biking kit and into a glorious hot shower. The shower was designed for two with six showerheads, two steam bath heads, and a large bench opposite the wide arched entrance. Since taking over the master suite with full spa and gym, Delores had enjoyed it amenities greatly. It was more peaceful than any resort spa, tucked away from distractions and noise without having to drive anywhere. The natural stone surfaces made it seem like she was showering in a hand-carved cave, and only the slight accent of blue tile around the main handle brought her back to modern day.

Refreshed, she went about her ritual of getting ready and went to select her clothing for the day. Nelda's newest staff member really had outdone herself in reorganizing the wardrobe room. Delores tended to dress in the same earth tones and fabrics from the same designers, yet now that the pieces had been arranged by exact shades there appeared to be greater variety. She chose the lightest of her natural linen blouses to wear open over a crisp turquoise tank and solid form fitting dark denim jeans.

She slid her feet into her natural cork sandals and walked quietly to the patio where the newspaper and hot coffee awaited. Once seated on her patio, Delores paused again to take in the beauty surrounding her. Newport Coast was a newer development in coastal Orange County, and at a five minute drive it was much further from the water than her father had lived for several decades. However, perched above natural shoreline the air was always crisp, and it was quite private. The estate offered the feel of a compound immediately upon driving through the iron gate at the road's edge. Neighbors could be reached, though most of them preferred to enjoy the privacy they had earned on the way to purchasing property for over $10 million.

Many of the owners employed full time staff to care for their needs, the grounds, and the home. At age 18 Nelda had started working for Juergen, and Delores could not imagine life without her. In fact, Nelda would present her with breakfast momentarily. She'd ask for her laptop as well. It was worth checking to see if she had any matches before greeting Ferdi and Polly.

After Nelda cleared her breakfast, she placed the charged laptop on the table for Delores. On the laptop she opened the matching service's site and navigated to:

Your Matches -> New Matches -> Matches Requesting Communication

It was the first time she looked at it, and several men had sent her notes. She looked at their personal summaries to decide if they were worth a response.

Jonathan from Orange, 48
Educational Sales
I like food, wine, and fast cars. Oh, and I like pretty women. I've always wanted to build a toy train set, and I've always wanted to travel the world, and it would be really cool to start a business. I've always wanted to write a book and be a professional musician. I'm just so much better at food, wine, and fast cars. And I love to spoil women, if you are that woman special enough to have my attention you will be really happy and we will have a great time.

How old could this Jonathan possibly be? He sounded like a child who never had accepted any responsibility. Educational sales may be his career, though it just seemed like his mentality would only allow for him to sell candy to children. Delores had an uneasy feeling about the childish man professing his interests in wine, fast cars, and pretty women while working in the education field. Delete.

Luke from Newport Beach, 46
Financial and Investment Advisor
I enjoy outdoor activities and spending time with my daughter. Keeping physically fit, skiing, going to the beach, flying a kite with my daughter, or simply spending some quality time together patiently answering endless questions little girls typically have. I love a good book, or going out to see a movie, or a concert. I also enjoy hanging out with my friends, and interesting conversations that often arise...

Luke sounded like a dedicated father if nothing else. Delores decided to keep him though she was not ready to respond to his questions. He could be an experiment if nobody more promising had written.

Marshall from Huntington Beach, 45
I own a fish tank cleaning bizness
I'm a walking contradiction: I eat very healthy AND I have a huge sweet tooth, I am a triathlete and exercise regularly AND I love to snuggle on the couch and watch movies, I work with people and talk for a living AND I enjoy quiet time by myself, I can sleep in the woods and forgo a shower for days AND I use facial moisturizer, I am a man of faith AND at times I find myself in fear, I am totally enough AND I want to be more, I am happy by myself AND I can't wait to find the love of my life!

Another man-child who must have been suffering from untreated ADHD. The thought of having this man clean her own fish tank was unsettling, much less establishing any possibility of sharing a water in the desert. She did not want to know his personal hygiene details in this forum. Did he smell like fish? There definitely was a problem with this matching system. Delete.

Micah from San Clemente, 37
Architect
If you're interested in a stereotypical male, I am not him. If you want to introduce each other to new exciting events, culture, arts, music, and ideas, Drop me a line. Oh and if you have a lust to travel to every corner of the Earth, I'm your man. Please email rather than send me some form of "hello." Thanks and happy hunting.

He started out promising. The slang was completely inappropriate. She had been warned about men who try to get women to communicate outside of the established structure of the site. For this reason Wendy had created the second account that would allow her to search anyone without a computer system validating his compatibility in advance. Delete.

Daniel from Long Beach, 42
Vice President at Non-Profit

I'm not sure how to judge the pictures posted online, but some people think I look younger than my age. I've been out of the dating scene for a while (the last relationship lasted a few years) and lost a few pounds since then. But jumping back in, it seems like everyone is really caught up in looks. I'm not sure how I stack up, but I think at least I used to be a good looking guy and girls liked me most of my life. I am a nice, honest, thoughtful man, and I am not interested in serial dateing. I'm not sure what this is all about, but it seems like it was worth a shot, so hopefully if I reach out you'll answer :)

Daniel, it was time to become a confident man. On what basis did the computer assume this match was compatible? Delete.

Chad from San Juan Capistrano, 49
Ophthalmologist
it's very important to me that in a relationship, my match and I take very good care of ourselves and our needs as individuals first and then the relationship provides the icing on the cake. In terms of time, I like the idea of spending time just the two of us, together with friends, separate with friends and alone. I think it provides balance or a well-rounded relationship and keeps other important relationships (including that with yourself) very healthy.

Chad said nothing about himself and seemed to cover only being alive and being healthy. If he could express himself better and learned to capitalize his sentences, she may consider him. Delete.

Larry from Newport Coast, 48
Entrepreneur
About me? Not yet, I'm pretty open about everything though. I like to be active. Kayaking, just tried stand up paddleboards love it, working out, hiking

Larry was even more elusive than Chad. Delores wondered briefly if Larry's profile was created on a mobile device or if he truly cared so little about the manner in which he was presenting himself to his matches. Perhaps women found his sense of mystery charming. If a man needed to produce such mystery in order to catch attention, though, Delores did not want to imagine the childish stunts he would pull once communicating. How could she take such a person seriously?

Delores pondered how much she was hiding in her profile. At least she and Wendy had taken the time to describe her honestly, and in a way that would allow her to remain a mystery. They were sure that after each encounter the man would always want more. Larry, however, contradicted himself by not telling anything, and then saying he was open. He had awful grammar. She considered that he might just be unintelligent. Goodness, she was amazed she just had spent so much time analyzing this dull man. It was appalling! Delete!

Karl from Newport Beach, 45
Lawyer (Acquisitions)
I am older than I look..... in a good way. Must be the lack of booze and good genes (mostly good...). It's good to be able to see my feet without a beer belly getting in the way and it will always stay this way. If you are looking for a drinking buddy.... look elsewhere. Don't care if you drink just as long as you don't have a drinking problem or "need" it to have fun.

Karl must have a drinking problem. The negativity was astounding! Delete.

Noah from Newport Coast, 44
sales and speaking
anyone who spends time with his grandfather must be a good guy (me). there is so much else to do but i like to be with my grandfather because he is such an incredible example of what a great man is to me - he is so loving toward my grandma, he is in incredible shape and still doing yard work at 91, he loves to explore and is always taking trips with my grandma, he is very caring and generous and donates his time to help others, he is intelligent and open to new ideas, he is accomplished and well off yet so humble you would never know, he gives great hugs and cries every time we say good bye (and he gets me every time!). He's the man and I love him dearly!

Delores couldn't believe the run-on sentences! She was not interested in dating a 91-year-old grandfather, and that was all Noah presented. Creative to some, perhaps. She found it an odd way of marketing and quite immature. It would be like her writing about Nelda. It was entirely irrelevant. Delete.

Henk from Newport Beach, 43
Financial Systems Manager
I'm looking for a woman who can leave her past relationships in the past and enter this relationship with warmth and an open heart. I have much to offer strength, kindness, warmth, depth, honesty and sincerity. I'm seeking a woman with the same values. We will be magical together you won't be disappointed, just leave your past in the past and get ready to discover what it is to be with a man who is not afraid of feelings.

Again, some may find this approach creative. She found it oddly creepy. Delete.

Hitting delete was becoming liberating. Delores was getting excited to delete her next pathetic match and just bring this entire experience to a close.

Maurice from Anaheim Hills, 48
Senior Account Executive
Limited texting is a good...Mr. Alexander Graham Bell invented phones for talking and returning calls. Everywhere you look, there are the zombies typing away as they drive, ride bikes, walk into telephone poles or into mall water fountains. Liberal voters can move along. Beside the socialist/redistributive economic policies helping to lead to financial ruin (hello Greece), just don't care for a pathological liar who spends more time being a wanna be celebrity than doing the job. He is clueless when off the teleprompter and can only resort to name calling and lies. What a pathetic arrogant little guy.

Perhaps Maurice forgot the purpose of this was to market himself to a woman to date, and not use it as a political chat room. Delores was surprised by this and Noah seemed much more sincere after Maurice's political rant. Irrelevant, and perhaps deeply disturbed. Delete.

Luis from Costa Mesa, 45
Engineer / Programmer
I am not Kreskin, so mind reading is not one of my talents. Unless they say something, have no idea what they think they notice since different people notice whatever they think they notice. Don't really care for making judgements within five seconds of meeting someone......that is quite superficial, no?

What? Luis definitely was not capable of clear thought. The grammar was minor compared to whatever the rest of his introduction included. Delete.

The delete key was beginning to feel like a lead weight. These people were just getting increasingly inappropriate. How had she thought this was a good idea? Two more messages remained, and she decided to read them.

Wendy had insisted that suitable matches were there, though they may require digging and patience. How had such clowns ever qualified for the site? Wendy had assured her it was highly distinguished among the competition. Delores was certain she would not have the patience to endure much more of this, and she would report that to Wendy by phone later this afternoon. There would be no written correspondence to associate her with this laughable investigation into the methods people so commonly used to find dates interested in marriage.

Drew from Irvine, 41
Commercial Banker (Medical Field)
A long list of what is important: staying close to family & friends, my career and continuing to achieve professional success, cycling, staying in shape (easier in CA than in Ohio for sure), being a good person who is thankful for what I have rather than what I

don't have, investing in the stock market and experiencing new things. I am definitely looking for a partner to share my life with who has similar morals, values and outlook on life.

At least Drew seemed like a real person finally. His profile picture, however, revealed an entirely unattractive man glistening with sweat. She clicked on the next picture and his sheen remained. She was not sure she could look at him, and she certainly couldn't imagine pretending to enjoy being close to him or absorbing his sweat. If he sweated that much without exertion, it made her stomach churn to think of his sweat simply walking across a room. And more than that? Okay, Luis, this was a 5 second judgment. Perhaps she was superficial. Drew was repulsive. Delete.

*A Flexible Match!***
***(A flexible match is someone who is highly compatible, yet does not meet one of your configurable preferences. Please give your match a chance! We think you will find many things in common!)*
Chandler from Nashville and La Jolla, 43
Cardiology Research and Education
I have created a legacy of my own design with my mind, and not with a trust fund. With abundant evidence of my commitment to self, goals, achievement, and contribution to society, I am ready to share my life with a partner who is intelligent, warm, and has achieved success outside standards known to the common individual. There must be a woman out there who is similar to me in sophistication, education, culture with an inherent knack for enjoying the simplest pleasures of life like the setting sun and flowers starting to bloom.

Maybe Wendy was right, Delores thought, or maybe she had been de-sensitized by the garbage she had spent the past 45 minutes sorting. Two locations was different, yet it applied to Delores as well since she had split her time among various cities. Chandler showed intelligence and sincerity. Was it odd that he liked flowers blooming? La Jolla was not entirely inconvenient. Chandler's appearance was definitely academic, and his body type also was quite rugged. This was an appealing combination. She clicked 'Answer His Questions' without further thought.

3 DELORES – TWO WEEKS AGO

The process had been clumsy at best for Delores, who felt that Chandler was an imaginary man whose statements and expressions were mirror images of her own. It had not seemed necessary to exchange personal telephone numbers as such information was the sort Delores liked to keep private. Instead, they were using the secure email feature from the online matching service. He was concise in his wording, and his communication was purposeful.

Since he was planning to return to Nashville in a few days, they had decided to meet for lunch prior to his departure. True to his word, he was a Southern gentleman and offered to meet in a location convenient to her even though it meant altering his return flight to depart from Orange County.

Choosing a location had been more difficult than she realized. It was important to her that they met in a public place where she could valet park her car and be recognized only enough for any sign of distress to be noticed by the staff. It would be like a business lunch, as though Chandler were vying for her business, yet she wanted to have a sexy flair.

She chose Newport Coast's signature resort and golf club that offered a public clubhouse and gorgeous view of the Pacific Ocean. They would meet at noon for a Sunday brunch, and she would visit her father immediately following the meal. She figured there was nothing to lose in the quick meeting, and if Chandler was interested in getting to know her he would have to accept the commute as necessary, regardless of the how much or little time they would spend together at each meeting.

Delores chose a turquoise raw silk dress with a fitted bodice and retro formed skirt. It was a perfect combination of sexy, sophisticated, and playful. Her three inch camel heels were classy and sexy without giving him the impression she had worn heels on his behalf. That only would be appropriate after several dates. She selected a camel cashmere scarf and simple camel suede clutch. Her makeup and hair were flawless as always, and Delores felt like a woman to be treasured as she made her way to her car.

She had been using a driver for transportation most of her life, and recent curiosity had pushed her to purchase an electric car. The Tesla Model S Signature Performance was a pleasure to drive, and she felt responsible owning one. With a range of several hundred miles, she had the option to get around on her own daily without ever having to think about gas. Nelda ensured one of the staff plugged it in for her so it always was ready. She smiled broadly as she navigated to the clubhouse forty minutes early.

Pedro greeted her eagerly at the clubhouse valet entrance. It had been some time since she had visited, and the staff welcomed her back as a treasured guest. All the arrangements for the brunch with Chandler on the green had been made.

Delores decided to remove her shoes and walk along the edge of the clubhouse green instead of taking a seat in the bar. Engaging in any conversation or mindless staring before Chandler arrived would be a waste of a perfectly wonderful morning.

To her surprise, as she was balancing on the stones of the lower green five minutes later, arms stretched out from her sides, she felt a strong hand on each arm. When she looked up she caught sight of Chandler. Startled, she chuckled. They had a lot in common after all.

She smiled. He fit like a glove.

He returned the smile and said, "Glenda, it is so nice to make your acquaintance."

4 MAIZIE – THREE WEEKS AGO

Maizie was in her new apartment in a the town of Laguna Beach, where she had just moved after coming to California for a new job in media relations with a lifestyle fitness clothing company. It was a huge change from her native Pennsylvania. In Laguna Beach, she was paying $6 per square foot for a space that was approximately as large as the master bedroom in her old apartment, and it was still over her budget. She didn't understand how people paid such prices for apartments, yet were still able to save up for multi-million dollar homes and drive exotic cars that cost more than she earned in a year.

Since her coworkers were mostly young and single, they all seemed to have extended their college phase by living with a bunch of other single people in flats that were walking distance to surf breaks, and, more importantly, a large selection of bars and pubs. Maizie was not interested in reliving or extending her student days. She had lived them. She accepted them for what they were. More importantly, she wanted to move on with her life as a career woman and enjoy the California sunshine to the fullest extent possible. She was young at heart and did not feel compelled to crawl on her knees to beg for her 20's back when she had grappled with turning 30 a full five years ago.

Finding her renovated apartment in the heart of town had taken three months. Living in the temporary housing her company had provided had become oppressive after only a couple of weeks, and she nearly had signed a lease on a dilapidated cottage by the sea to escape. It was charming, but the landlord was a little creepy. It was just ridiculous to find a place in her price range, though. She combed the ads and waited.

The corporate extended suite in Lake Forest was far from the paradise she had imagined and found along the Orange County coast. Staying at the suites there had been entertaining moments and also some that caused her to doubt her decision to move to California. Her family and friends definitely were right about the bizarre and crazy people she would encounter in her new environs.

One day during her third week at the hotel a sudden shaking, blaring fire alarm, alarm strobe lights, and foul odor of water from sprinklers shocked Maizie out of a deep slumber. The entire building was evacuated. She stood in her robe with her laptop in its neoprene sleeve (thankfully she was religious about storing it properly), bare feet, without her contact lenses, from 3 am until dawn broke. Everyone waited for the fire squad to extinguish the fire that resulted from a fellow guest's methamphetamine lab explosion. He was clueless about what was going on around him, likely high.

Maizie wished she could have seen what the others were describing as the stunned, long haired man standing naked in the window of his suite drinking from a mug as though it was a normal day. It was anything but normal as smoke billowed around him, fire blazed behind him, and two members of the fire squad climbed a ladder to retrieve him. It must have looked like a strange religious exhibition for a cult or something.

Everyone else was stuck in the parking lot without refreshments. Sure, it was slightly entertaining to see the criminal wrapped in a silver-colored plastic sheet, read his rights, and placed in the back of a squad car to the Lake Forest police station. The fact of the matter was an entire wing of the hotel had been destroyed by the malfunction of his drug production equipment. Everything the guests of that wing owned that had been in their suites had been destroyed. She had wondered if renter's insurance would cover her losses, and more importantly what she would wear to work, how to replace her car key, and if her box of diaries would be salvageable.

That morning Maizie decided she would never again put herself in the situation where such low class people could live near her. The whole thing made her sick. She decided she would do whatever it took to live in a high class, peaceful neighborhood where she would be proud to invite guests. There had been too many years of living below her desired standard so that she could save for a nice home, and now nothing was left of that money. It didn't look like she'd have enough for a house out on this coast, so she would be forced to spend more on rent than originally anticipated. It would stretch her budget, and given the alternative she didn't care.

She became extremely picky. Any apartment she would consider was required to have granite counters, custom cabinetry, smooth walls without cracks, high ceilings, natural light, wood floors, a newly renovated bathroom that included glass shower doors, and not be in a complex. She wanted it to feel like a house. She did not want it to be a cookie cutter place that she could find in Pennsylvania. It had to be just for her.

She had decided on Laguna Beach because it had seemed the most exclusive of the beach cities while still offering a place for someone with less wealth to live comfortably. Homes had been built into the cliffs along the beach and up to the top of the hills on the opposite side of the coast highway. What most homes had in common was a view of the ocean, and the median price was $2.6 million. It was a quiet town, and even rentals proved to be exclusive.

Renovated one-bedroom rentals started at $1,800 monthly, and neither a parking space nor private laundry facility was guaranteed at that price. When she finally spotted the listing for her place, Maizie knew that it was her next home. She replied by email to the post immediately.

She waited an entire afternoon. Finally, the response came back that the unit had been rented to another applicant. Maizie would not accept that. She pressed on and wrote about her interests and credentials, and all the work that had just gone into cover letters in her job hunt paid off. The owner admitted she had fibbed about the unit being rented, stating that she actually had decided on a renter from a pool of over a dozen highly qualified renters.

After exchanging 27 emails with the owner, who refused to give her phone number, the owner had been won over and agreed to rent the unit to Maizie. This was especially remarkable since Maizie did not even have enough money for a deposit of nearly $4,000 due to be postmarked within 96 hours, and the owner knew this. Maizie said she would find it, and she did.

Now she was enjoying the setting immensely. There were only two neighbors, and they were quite friendly. She greeted each in passing and exchanged the polite couple sentences of idle cordiality on occasion. Maizie knew she would not become close friends with them, though. That would be too much like having roommates. She wanted her own space, period. Plus these neighbors seemed uneducated. As her father would say, they live in flip-flops and do not want any more from life.

Maizie put on her flip-flops, locked the door behind her, and set off to take a stroll along the beach to admire all that she soon would have. She lived on a hill that overlooked the main street into and out of town and the highway that ran along the coast. A set of stairs led to town, so she could walk to anything she needed. A market, hair salon, liquor store, spa, boutiques, bars, pharmacies, banks, and restaurants were a few minutes away on foot. She could also turn right at the bottom of the steps and venture to the beach in less than two minutes. It was pure heaven. She didn't care that she lived in a shoebox while her friends in Pennsylvania all had pools larger than her apartment.

Every night she took a walk at sunset and posted a photo of the beautifully colored clouds and illuminated ocean to her Facebook page. Those pool people were all jealous. They would comment that they wished they could live in paradise or joke about trading places for a day. In truth she envied that so many of her friends were so much further in their lives both financially and in terms of relationships. She had never married. Actually, she had never considered marrying any of the men she dated. She attracted more men than 20 of her friends combined, and for some reason they just didn't do it for her. They were boring.

She wanted more. If there was such a thing as soul mates, she was sure she had met hers already at an age that made it impossible to develop a relationship, so her chance had passed. Jared. Until they were 12 they spent every waking moment together building forts, playing video games, riding bikes, and swimming. He ignored her with determination at school, and she knew it was because he was embarrassed to like her and afraid of being teased. Everyone knew her mom was in and out of the psych ward and her dad was a drunken lunatic who should be stuck in jail. Then one day after school, when they had just mastered the newest Ninja Man video game, Jared nonchalantly told her that his family was moving to Texas the next day.

It was an awkward parting. She wanted to kiss him. He was the only boy she ever wanted to kiss until then. His name, her name with his last name, and all sorts of dreamy love notes filled the pages of three diaries in the drawer of her desk at home. He was the love of her life, and she wanted to cry and beg him not to go.

Instead she had said, "Cool, well, bye, I guess."

"Yeah, cool."

That was it. Her life had changed forever. That was the last of Jared.

Then two months ago she had run into him at a music festival. Her entire body had become energized, alert and screaming at her that she was looking at the man of her dreams even before they acknowledged each other. Her body remembered him. A crush of over 20 years once again became a possibility to her.

He caught her gaze and stopped what he was saying so his mouth hung open. His face was frozen for several seconds before his eyes sparked and a giant smile framed perfectly straight white teeth. He stepped away from whomever he'd been talking to and rushed to her.

"Maizie Miller? Is that really you? What are you doing here?" He hugged her. He was beaming and chuckling with disbelief at this unlikely reunion.

Immediately she wanted to tell him she missed him and had always hoped they would run into each other. She wanted to put him in a box, take him home with her, and keep him in her closet to pull out whenever she wanted to see him. She never wanted to let him go. She had to keep him.

19

"Jared! Wow. Hey. How are you?"

She grinned. She may have even blushed. She was acting like a stupid teenager. Worse. She was acting like she was 12 years old again. He would not believe that she had a hip and responsible position as a media relations manager. She smiled and waited for him to answer. She had been the last person to speak, so it was his turn. She wanted to know everything about his life and what he'd been doing for the last 23 years. He wasn't speaking.

He just smiled. He must have felt the same way. She had always known he was crazy about her and he just didn't know what to do about it. It must be shocking to him, too, to have the woman of his dreams standing right there in front of him, and to have just hugged. They'd never hugged before, and she was in awe of how magical this moment was. It was meant to be. She knew it.

He still wasn't speaking. Come on, Jared, talk!

"It's you. How are you?" she asked.

"Awesome. I can't believe it's you, Maizie! Well, hey, my band is like going to play in about like 20 minutes. Can you like stick around and listen? We've like been really jamming with like new songs lately. You'll dig it, and we can like catch up later. Cool?"

"Wow, you're in a band? What do you play?"

"I've been like on backup vocals, for, like, a couple months now, and like I'll pick up a guitar sometimes, too. It's sweet. I like even have a card." He reached into his pocket and handed her the business card he pulled out of it. "Cool, huh? You can, like, look up our web page and everything. It's like really my part time job, but, hey, like I really want to like take it to the next level, you know? So like are you gonna stay?"

"Yes. Definitely," she said. "I'll text you now so you have my number, too." She knew her smile was stretching from ear to ear.

"Cool, well, hey, I'm gonna like head backstage and like get set up. I like can't believe you're gonna like hear me play, Maizie! Awesome!" Jared leaned over and planted a quick kiss on her cheek and headed across the parking lot to the main stage.

Maizie couldn't believe it either. Jared had been her crush in middle school, and now not only had he kissed her but he also was a rock star. This was incredible. She had fantasies as a child of being forgotten by her parents at a concert, and then the rock star would find her and take her home in a limo. He'd tell her she was special and invite her to come to all of his shows on the East Coast because she was so important.

Now she was watching Jared perform in California. Maybe the fantasy would come true after all, but without the parents forgetting her. In fact, it was without the parents entirely. This was so much better! His parents couldn't take him away again, and hers couldn't embarrass her.

She was so happy to be with Jared again. He really had become

Californian. He talked like a stoned surfer, and she found it endearing. She remembered that she used to get out of her desk and crawl between desks until she was under his in order to give him the answers for all their tests in school. She was sure he still was smart, though. He just wasn't very fast, and she was always done so far in advance of anyone else.

Maizie found a spot where she could watch him clearly. He looked so handsome on stage. He had grown to about six feet tall. His brown hair was just longer than his ears, and his blue eyes glowed with amazing passion as he sang. The music was not great, and she didn't care. It was a cover of a popular female artist whose songs were about bitter relationships and drug addiction. It was very ambitious for this band of hipster-grunge young men. He had an incredible vocal range, and he kept looking at her and smiling. She was sure he was singing just for her.

Maizie examined the card Jared had given her. It was not professional, and she did not understand how they thought it would promote them or make them memorable unless they were looking to offend. It was the color of cedar, and the band's name was spelled out in white foam: Sick Suck. She knew from her involvement in the surf and skate scene that this was a reference to surfing. The band had selected a cheap reprographics shop that made it look like semen on skin rather than sea foam on sand. Jared's intelligence, or lack thereof, again entered her mind. She would have to talk to him about this card. It was the perfect reason to text him so he would have her number.

'I can introduce your band to a printer. I'm so happy to hear you play. Maizie'

Sick Suck played a set that seemed to last a lifetime, and then they finally finished. Maizie slowly glided over toward the stage, where Jared was wrapping up cords from the equipment. Before she reached him, a lean woman made her way to the stage, hopped up, and sat down at a slight angle so she effectively blocked Jared and ensured that only she could talk to him.

This woman looked like pure white trash with a slightly off skin tone, frizzy hair with too much styling product, and jeans that may have been new but were cut to a style that had gone out of style 10 years ago. It was not the type of hipster-retro that worked. It looked cheap. The white trash woman was trying to possess Jared. She was like a wild cat, leaping up there and threatening to lash out with her claws if any other woman so much as looked at Jared.

Maizie was unimpressed, though quite aware of the competition. She slowed her pace and stood to the backside of the white trash cat woman so she would not initiate a catfight. Jared was smiling while talking to the cat woman, and then noticed Maizie. He crossed the stage and jumped down, passing in front of the cat woman to approach Maizie.

"You guys sounded really great up there!" she told him as he approached.

He hugged her again, this time pressing close to her and holding her tight.

"Thanks, Maizie Miller! Ha! It is like such a trip that you are here. Do you, like, live in California now? You, ah, you like look great."

She laughed, making sure to show off her perfectly aligned teeth that matched the whites of her eyes exactly. This was a trick that her dentist used to ensure perfect balance of her features, which were striking already. When she smiled with those teeth and her blue eyes lit up, no man could resist melting into her spell.

She was a blonde by birth, and her hair was always naturally glossy. It flowed down to the middle of her back in gentle waves that most women would die to have. It was hers naturally. There was more competition in her new home, surely, but Maizie knew that most of these women paid the price in time and money to resemble what was hers for free. This left more time for Maizie to hunt for men.

The body of a swimsuit model complemented her beautiful face, and for this she did have to work. Maizie would participate in any land-based sport when the opportunity arose, and it was at the gym with a personal trainer that she found the most satisfaction. She loved being pushed to the brink of passing out from exhaustion. She loved being driven further and further each session, and the smug validation from the trainer shaking his head in disbelief at her incredible physical capabilities and depth of her determination. The result of her hours in the gym was a body that looked impeccable from any angle.

Since she worked for a lifestyle fashion company, Maizie's wardrobe did not require endless hours of shopping, an activity she regarded as a waste of time. She had the latest in active wear, and often took home pieces that had yet to be released. The white cotton shorts she was wearing had a 1" inseam that showed off her smooth athletic legs and sculpted rear. Her flat stomach, perfectly proportioned chest, and feminine shoulders were highlighted beautifully in her hip-length tailored blue and red plaid blouse. She had snapped it closed only in the center. She was the sexiest lady around, and she knew it. Yes she looked great. She always did.

"I just moved here for a new job. I love it. What about you?"

"Oh, yeah, well I like came out here to like visit a friend from Texas when he was like going to school in San Diego, and, uh, I like picked up a surfboard and have been like totally hooked for like a dozen years now. I just like couldn't go back to Texas, you know, so like I just stayed in San Diego and like made my way up here. You know it's like totally the typical story. Ma and Pops are like totally pissed and all cuz they like want me to be there and give them like a bunch of grandkids and stuff. You know? But I love it here, you know? So, hey, do you want to like maybe grab a drink or something sometime? I'd like really like to catch up, you know, if you like have time and all."

Maizie smiled with her lips pressed together, so the effect was mischievous and seductive. "Of course. My schedule is pretty busy, but I can make a little time I'm sure. Here, I'll give you my number and just let me know when you were thinking."

"Uh, you like already texted me so I like have your number. So, cool, I'll get in touch sometime."

Again, he wrapped his arms around her, kissed her cheek, and dashed back to the stage where the cat woman was eagerly awaiting his return with diminishing patience that revealed her insecurities. Maizie made eye contact with the cat woman and held her gaze, expressionless, for five full seconds before moving away. The cat woman must have surmised that Maizie was not one who played to lose. At anything. Ever.

5 MAIZIE – TWO MONTHS AGO

Jared was taking his time calling. It had been two weeks since she ran into him at the music festival, and still he hadn't called. She knew he was thinking of her. He had to be. How could he not? Was he seriously dating that white trash cat woman in the awful stonewashed jeans? Gross. She decided to give him a little encouragement. Picking up her cell phone, she texted him a quick hello.

'Jared, great to see you. I have tickets to a concert at the park by Balboa Pier this Friday at 7. Want to go? Maizie'

Okay, now she could go about her day dealing with the photographers who wanted to post pictures from a surf trip to Tahiti in a skate magazine. She kept arguing about the cross-pollination being ineffective, and they kept ignoring her. They were "epic" pictures, and she would use them somewhere that would be appropriate to the audience and timing. It did not matter what they thought. They would have to learn to live with her decisions.

After work, Maizie went to a nearby gym knowing it would be full, as always, of meatheads and bimbos pumping iron and trying to pick up someone new. To her the gym had always been purely for exercise, but she was beginning to enjoy the attention that was showered on her by the men. Most of them only looked. A few would invent excuses to talk to her or ask about what weight she was using for her exercises.

One guy silently offered to wipe down the treadmill she was climbing onto a few weeks ago, and then reappeared to do the same when she'd completed her run. He must have been watching her the whole time. She liked that. She grew to expect this service from the quiet gentleman.

Tonight after her run the wiping man caught up with her after he wiped down her treadmill.

"Hi," said the man who only had smiled previously.

She noticed that he actually was a perfect height for her. His defined chest was directly at her eye level, and it was nice to look at. "Hi, yourself," she said, not ready to look directly at him.

"I keep seeing you around, and I really wanted to introduce myself. My name is Hank."

"Does every new girl in town get the same service, Hank?"

Maizie kept walking.

Hank froze for a moment, and then followed her toward the weights.

Hank was actually rather handsome. He had a strong jaw line, ruddy tan, and thick auburn stubble that had a light salt and pepper that was streaked through his full head of auburn hair. His hair was cut nicely, like he appreciated a job done well. His eyes were somewhere between hazel and green, and they showed a sincerity that she hadn't seen on the West Coast yet.

"Where are you from, Hank?"

"I live in Laguna Beach. I grew up in Boston, and moved here a couple years ago. You just look like a very interesting person. I know that sounds cliche, doesn't it? It's just that I'm really interested in getting to know you."

"Well, Hank, what do you want to know?"

She was struggling not to smile. He was really falling over himself to ask her out. She loved this part.

"Would you join me for lunch on Saturday?"

She was impressed at his sudden ability to find his balls and be decisive.

"Hmmm. I don't really know you, Hank."

She smiled and thought he must be dying as she turned up the level of difficulty to get her to go out with him. At the same time she knew she looked irresistible.

"Javier's at Crystal Cove. On the patio. One-thirty. You won't regret it."

Hank seemed quite certain of himself. She had not even introduced herself.

"I'll think about it."

She knew she would go. He was really cute. He was a perfect distraction.

"Okay, Maizie. I won't be here to service your equipment the next couple days, so I'll see you Saturday."

Maizie's smile shifted to indicate a slight surprise that he knew her name. He was already halfway across the room, and he was growing on her a little. Hank was full of surprises. Jared wasn't taking the bait of the concert tickets, so she may as well go out for a harmless lunch with Hank. At least he might take her mind off Jared. She wondered if Jared really was thinking about her, and then her mind was once again consumed by the weights in her hands as she imitated the workouts prescribed by her trainer back East.

When she returned to the extended suites, Maizie was pleased to see that Jared had replied to her text.

'Hey Maizie. Luv 2 :) grab drink b4 @ cantina next 2 park?'

'Yes. See you Friday.'

She didn't understand California sometimes. Why was a grown man texting like a teenager? Well, she had him for Friday. Now she just had to get the tickets.

Friday night approached fast, and the tickets had been hard to find. Apparently some local kid had made it big in the European jazz scene and was returning for a special hometown performance. He would take the audience on a musical journey of his coming of age and dealing with success, failure, traveling, and encounters with foreigners as he adapted to life in Paris. Or something like that. Newport Beach was so pretentious.

Why did they always have such elaborate explanations for something that was going to be a sellout anyway? She guessed it was compulsory to print all the material so people would have something to tell their friends about the music other than, "It was jazz" or "It was good". This was the emotional journey of a jazz musician, and she was positive that Jared would love it.

Maizie arrived at the cantina a few minutes before six and took in her surroundings. The paint was bright colors with glossy finish, and there were stools scattered around small tables. A bar ran the length of the back wall, so the patrons looked at alcohol bottles and had a peek-a-boo view of the Pacific Ocean from a single window in the rear corner. She would have done it differently, but it was not her bar.

She ordered a margarita and took a seat at the window. She could gaze at the ocean while waiting for Jared and see everyone entering and exiting the cantina. If it was her bar, she would have a full wall of windows behind the bar, so everyone would enjoy the view of the park, ocean, and people passing on the boardwalk as they drank, not even thinking about how many they had consumed. It would be great business for the bar, and everyone would be happy to enjoy the scenery. She was certain the owner and manager were neither visual nor interested in creating a space people would love. They wanted the quantity of patrons their liberal happy hours guaranteed to bring.

Three margaritas and 45 minutes later, Maizie was about to text Jared to let him know she was at the cantina when he strolled in the door carrying a black motorcycle helmet. He was wearing loose jeans that sat low on his hips with a studded black belt, tight vintage blue V-neck t-shirt, and a leather jacket designed for aerodynamics and protection in case of contact with asphalt. His hair flowed gently over his eyes. Scanning the room, he shook back his head to get the hair out of his eyes, and smiled sheepishly when he spotted her.

"Maizie, hi," he said as he moved close to hug her. "How's it going?"

"Hi, Jared."

She never would have stayed around for any other guy, but she was rather certain that he was worth the wait. Plus she had been craving the feeling of his arms around her for the entire two weeks that they'd been apart.

"You ride?"

"Oh, yeah, I like got a bike a few years ago cuz it's like so much easier to like get around, you know. I'm like super stoked about the concert. Thanks for like inviting me."

Maizie realized her father would not appreciate Jared's English. Her father had corrected her so many times when she was a teen. "Is it 'like 75 degrees out' or is the temperature 75 degrees?" he would ask. She learned to abide by proper grammar and usage, and it had been an incredible advantage in her career.

"You're welcome. It seems like it is already time to walk over and take our seats."

"Oh, yeah, I like totally lost track of time earlier. I was like jamming out some new songs with the band and like totally just like fell asleep when I went home to like change. So we can like get a few drinks after if you're like not in a hurry or whatever."

"I'd like that." In fact all that she liked about the evening was the chance to be close to Jared.

After the concert Jared, who had enjoyed it immensely, asked Maizie if she'd like to go to a bar closer to his house for a drink. He wanted to be able to walk home. She teased him for being so responsible, and agreed to go along with that plan. She was going to follow him and park at his house, and they'd walk over together.

He lived in a nicer part of town than his demeanor would suggest. Driving down the tree-lined streets atop the hill in Newport Beach, he pulled into the driveway of a sprawling two-story craftsman. Maizie parked along the curb as he'd instructed her, and stepped onto the street. Jared was by her side before she reached the curb.

"Damn, you're like fancy Maizie in your sporty little Mini Cooper. Is that like a custom paint job? It's sweet!"

"Thanks. It's custom soda blue paint with steel leather interior. I'm in lifestyle fashion, so it's important to stay current on all the trends. It is not unlike you with music."

"Uh, I guess. I sorta just play like what the band wants. I like really dug the dude tonight. So you wanna like come into my place so we can like play a video game like old times? I have like a few kinds of wine and some beer or whatever if you're like really interested in a drink."

"Are you sure your girlfriend wouldn't mind?"

Maizie loved using this line. It was accepting an invitation and finding out his status at the same time.

He laughed, which she took as a good sign.

"What makes you like think I have a girlfriend? I'm like out with you on like a Friday night, right? Come on, doll."

Perfect. She had no interest in the video game, but getting inside his house would open all the doors that did interest her. He put his arm around her and she leaned into him in a fluid motion, as though they had years of practice walking as a couple. She wondered how long it would take for him to kiss her. She was certain a kiss was coming very soon. He was obviously smitten with her.

She couldn't help but run through the names in her head: Maizie Miller Portrell. Jared and Maizie Portrell. Mrs. Portrell. It was intoxicating. She was so excited. They hadn't talked much, and she didn't feel the need to catch up with words. All that mattered was they were together and he was leading her into his home. At first she expected him to have roommates in such a large place, but it was silent when they entered.

The mess could have been made by a group of fraternity guys, but it all seemed to be his. He didn't excuse the condition of the house, leading her to believe that he was accustomed to this state of disarray. He led her across the entry and into the game room, where they sat on the overstuffed brown sofa that was situated five feet from a 55" television mounted to the wall.

"Jared, look at you with this amazing house! Amazing. And yet there's still the kid side of you!"

"Oh, yeah, Pops like thought it would be good as like an investment. I rent it from him, you know, and then like they have a place to stay when they're here. Ma like cooks me all sorts of food so I like don't have to worry about it when they're not here. They come out like four or five times a year. It's a chill pad though. It like totally beats the mess at the beach. All that sand, you know? And he like charges me almost no rent. What about you? Where do you like live and all?"

"I'm looking for the right spot still. I want to live by the ocean. I was thinking any place within a half mile of the ocean between Newport Beach and Laguna Beach would be fine. It is a tough market."

"Boyfriend?"

"Oh, Luke. He's on the East Coast still. I'm pretty sure he won't be coming out. He wants to. It seems more and more like we were drifting apart, so this might be a good excuse to just end it."

There was no Luke. There was no boyfriend. She just wanted to feel out his interest.

"Ah, so like you do have a boyfriend. I totally thought so. How could you not? You're like totally hot. Way out of my league if like I didn't like already know you."

"What about you? What's going on in your love life?"

He held up both hands, "You're looking at it." He chuckled. "Nah, I am like dating four or five chicks right now, but like, obviously nobody that I want to like make a commitment to or anything, you know? I just, like, enjoy hanging out with some, and well, like, well with some it's more than just hanging out, you know?"

"Oh, sure. I totally agree. I mean, why would you commit to a woman who wasn't what you really wanted? You're young and handsome and an aspiring musician. The drama of a woman you don't love would be a big distraction."

"Uh, yeah, or it could like give me some really good material. I like to write songs, and I just like don't have the greatest imagination or something to like make a hit. Nothing has ever really like happened to me. I just like want to write."

"I am sure you will be very good at it. I don't even know the lyrics to most of the music I listen to. If the music is good, then the words don't matter as much. You just need a beat that can keep the ear interested for a few minutes. That's all. You don't need to be like the guy from tonight's concert."

"Yeah, I guess you're right. My parents think I have to like be the next like Neil Diamond or something, with songs everyone like sings in the shower, in the car, and like wherever they are. They like really want me to 'grow up and settle down'. They want grandkids, and like bring it up all the time, you know. I definitely don't want to get married now. I'm just not interested in like all that stuff. I really don't want a serious relationship now either. That's for sure. I make that, like, really clear before I even kiss a girl."

Maizie sensed that he was getting very agitated discussing the expectations that he felt his parents had of him. She put her hand on his knee.

"Jared, it is your life. They want you to be happy, and they don't want to you forget about their own dreams for you. Take your time. There is no hurry."

He looked at Maizie with her big eyes. There was a depth he could just jump into with all he had, never having to worry about where he was falling because it appeared there was no bottom. He was hypnotized. He took a deep breath, and instead of letting the tension out he reached out with his left hand, grabbed her behind the neck, and pulled her to him. All of the tension that had been coursing through him seconds ago was transformed into passion, and she wholeheartedly returned the kiss.

She moaned lightly, and he lifted her off the couch and set her on his lap facing him. She pressed her chest to his and started to move her hips just enough so he was fully aware of her. She pulled back from his lips and moved her neck across his face gently, curving her head to brush her lips across his neck and nibble softly at his ear.

"Maizie," he moaned.

It was all over. He had no defense to her scent and her lips. He lifted her off his lap so she stood in front of him. He clumsily unbuttoned her skinny jeans, pulled down the zipper, and rested his hands on her hips, just staring at the thin lace fabric of her underpants for a moment. He turned his hands up so his fingers could grasp the waistband and pull both garments to the floor.

She was running her hands through his hair, and he could hardly contain his excitement. She stepped one foot at a time out of her bottoms, and pulled at his t-shirt slowly. He lifted his arms, and allowed her to pull it over his head. She threw it across the room carelessly as his hands fell back onto her hips.

He wanted to touch every part of her body. She was so hot. He had to get his pants off right away. He had to get inside her. He had never been so turned on in his life, and he had been with a lot of women. Nothing like Maizie. He wanted to touch her and he wanted to be inside her. He couldn't decide what to do so he just kept his hands on her hips until she pulled his face straight ahead and buried it in her crotch. She lifted a leg over his shoulder and he moaned as he kissed her delicately. She clenched her hands in his hair and screamed out as he quickly brought her to climax.

He pulled his face back and they both chuckled. He still wanted her. It was time to see and feel more of her. He quickly moved his hands to her chest, and ran them down to her waist, feeling the gorgeous curves. Jared unbuttoned her blouse slowly, starting at the bottom and working his way up. He didn't dare look her in the eyes again, or he knew he'd turn into a savage beast and it would be over in 10 seconds. This was so hot. He wanted it to last. He wanted this to remain the hottest sex of his life.

When he reached the top button, he gently pushed her shirt off her shoulders, still staring at her chest and flat stomach. She was so hot. He reached behind to unclasp her bra, and she released a sexy, intoxicating chuckle as he struggled for a minute with it. He had to focus on taking a deep breath as he finally got it unclasped, and slowly pulled it toward him off her arms.

His hands were lined up perfectly to stroke her stomach and cup her gorgeous breasts in his hands. He moved his hands gently over her breasts, admired their perfection, and with the same sudden movement as the kiss he stood up and pressed his lips to her right breast. He caressed her left breast with his hand and attacked her right one with his mouth.

He had to get his pants off and let his enormous erection loose. Maizie was moaning in pleasure. He moved his left hand from behind the small of her back to rest behind her neck and head. He felt her press her head back into his hand, and he was about to lose himself.

Deep breath.

She was so hot.

He could hardly take it.

He pressed his mouth harder to her chest, and she cried out in pleasure. He was about to burst. He had to get his pants off. He had never been so distracted on the way to getting inside a woman. He realized he was standing and could drop his pants to the floor in a second. But that would mean he'd have to let go of her breast or her head.

He moved his mouth to her left breast, and she again cried out in pleasure and pressed herself to him. He knew she felt him hard against her, and he had to push her away slightly to unbutton his jeans. He couldn't wait a second longer.

"God, Maizie..." he whispered.

He pulled his pants and boxers to the floor. His face was again at eye level with her crotch. He buried his face in it, turning her around at the same time and using his arms to lay her down on the sofa. He didn't take his lips away for a second. It felt like she was about to climax again, and he wanted to feel it. He wanted to be inside her.

She made a faint moaning sound, and he quickly moved on top of her and thrust himself in. She yelled out as she came, and instantly he came and screamed in ecstasy. He wanted to stay right where he was. He wanted her again. He fell asleep.

He kept waking up hard and taking her again. Then he woke up hard and she was not there. Shit, was he dreaming or had he really taken Maizie Miller last night? He jerked off thinking of her and fell asleep again.

Maizie got out of bed just after 11 am. After leaving Jared's as dawn broke, she had hit the gym before climbing into her bed at extended stay. She couldn't believe that she'd actually spent the night with Jared Portrell. He definitely was into her. She was sure that she would be the one to change his mind. She was sure that he would want to commit to her. From her spot on the treadmill, she thought about how he could hardly contain himself from the second she placed her hand on his leg.

Maizie had always been amused at how well she could stimulate multiple senses in a man. Allowing them to smell just a light signature scent was a trick her father had taught her. Among the other girl training lessons, given by her slurring drunk father, was the one of wearing just enough perfume for her date to be able to catch a hint of it at the end of the night. She was certain he had not intended for it to be turned to her use of it, and grateful for the tip nonetheless.

She was a little disappointed in Jared's prowess. Still, she knew he would be trainable. He definitely had potential, and he had been very keen on pleasing her. It seemed to bring him pleasure. Her favorite part, as always, was when he said, "God, Maizie." Jared had said that before he was inside her. That was even better. He definitely wanted her. She would have him.

And the sex would get better. It wasn't bad, by any means, but it would become incredible. And she would move into his house and become his wife. He would never look at another woman again because she would always be the hottest thing he had ever imagined. If he imagined more, she would surpass his expectations. She had even left so that he would wake up wanting more and thinking about her. She would have him.

After working out, she was able to get solid sleep for five hours before it was time to get ready for lunch with Hank. Until Jared was committed to her, she was determined to eat up as much attention as she could from other men. In fact, several relationship experts insisted that only dating multiple men simultaneously would allow the desired man to end the chase and commit. Mrs. Jared Portrell. It sounded dreamy to her ears as she said it out loud. She would marry a rock star.

Maizie sang in the shower, still intoxicated from the night she'd spent with Jared. It was just having him that excited her so much. Nothing had entered his mind other than her on his journey to get inside her over and over again. It wouldn't take much to get Hank on the same track. All she had to do was show up for lunch.

Maizie arrived at Javier's at 1:15 and investigated the restaurant. She was wearing a short skirt that accentuated her shapely butt and legs and a blue and white chevron patterned t-shirt that slouched off her shoulder and draped casually across her chest. Her sandals had a rope-wrapped four-inch heel and helped enhance the appeal of her lean and evenly proportioned body.

After peering into each room of the restaurant, she was confident of her place in it and went to the ladies' room to touch up her makeup. Here at Javier's, she decided, she wanted to attract more eyes than Hank's. The restaurant felt rich. Everyone was dressed beautifully, groomed with attention to detail, and emanating health and wealth. The air coming off the ocean a few hundred yards away and the flames on the patio made it seem like she had been transported to another world. It was exclusive. This crowd was willing to pay $25 for a burrito, and that was the kind of man she wanted to have feast on her.

At 1:28 Maizie left the ladies' room and took slow, exaggerated steps toward the patio to meet Hank at their table. He was wearing jeans and a light gray polo shirt that showed a tiny bit of chest hair. His shoes and watch appeared to be expensive, which was always a good indication to Maizie that the man respected himself through the details of his appearance.

Jared was a lot more casual, but he also clearly dressed to whom he was. He was a musician and creative type, and he rode a motorcycle. His shoes had to be more functional than high end. He didn't care about time other than keeping a beat, as he'd proven by being late last night. He was free spirited. He could get away with it because she was crazy about him, and he didn't need to work hard to maintain a high standard of living as long as he lived in the house his parents essentially had bought for him. There were not a lot of Jared's. Hank had to work harder, and she knew he was aware of this by how he presented himself.

Hank stood as she approached, "Hi, Maizie."

She returned his smile and playfully exaggerated her last couple steps even more so he could admire her legs.

"Hi."

Hank pulled out her chair like a true gentleman and returned to his own seat. She was facing the ocean, and he was facing her. She figured each of them was happy with their respective view. Hank, previously so quiet, was rather conversational over lunch. He wanted to know everything about her, so she came to believe he had meant what he said at the gym. He was interested in getting to know her.

She didn't care much about Hank, so she continued to answer his questions with a degree of honesty that surprised her. She was just so distracted by thoughts of Jared that she couldn't concentrate on playing coy, hard to get, or any other role except saying whatever came to mind first. Startled by this, she decided to ask Hank questions instead. She paid no attention to what he was saying. She made sure to nod, laugh, and touch his hand at the appropriate time, but she was not present to him. All that was going through Maizie's mind was Jared.

After four margaritas and a shrimp and crab burrito, Maizie was ready to end the lunch date. Hank, ever the gentleman, escorted her to the valet, paid her ticket, and gave her a hug with a kiss on the cheek. He held her a slight distance from himself.

"Maizie, I really enjoyed getting to know you a bit. Would you consider joining me for dinner tomorrow night at Nick's in Laguna Beach?"

"Hank, tomorrow isn't good for me. I want to see you again, though. You'll be at the gym this week, right?"

He laughed.

"You really are a piece of work, Maizie. Yes, I'll be at the gym Monday at 5:30 to wipe down your treadmill and beg for the pleasure of your company over a meal very soon."

Jared still hadn't called her by Monday. No text. No evidence that he cared about her or wanted her again. Maizie was puzzled by his detachment. Last time it had taken two weeks, and she had initiated contact. Would she have to reach out and pull him in again? This was not what she was used to from men. She was used to them falling all over her and fighting to fend them off. She would have Jared.

She had to get Jared out of her mind. She had not been able to get anything done all day at work because she was daydreaming of Jared and imagining conversations that would take place with him. They had hardly spoken, yet in her head it seemed like she was getting to know what made him tick.

When she got to the gym, Hank greeted her at her treadmill. Hank would be her distraction from Jared. She tried to embrace it, and it took a lot of energy. All she saw was Jared with his hands on her hips, wondering what he was supposed to do with the woman of his dreams. She was high from the thought that she had so much power over him.

Where was he? She knew he would be his. Maizie ran with determination and was totally exhausted after 55 minutes on the treadmill. She had a runner's high from the exertion, and Hank appeared in seconds to wipe down the machine.

"Okay, Maizie, when can I take you to dinner? I want spend time with you."

"Hank, tonight is your lucky night. Are you available in an hour?" She knew he would rearrange anything if it were presented as a one-time shot. "Otherwise I'm booked until Friday."

"Okay. I'll pick you up in an hour. What is your address?"

"No. I appreciate the offer, but I'll meet you at Nick's in an hour."

It felt really good to be back on her game. She wanted to hold onto the runner's high, and this new plan for dinner was helping with that.

Maizie had all she needed to look hot for Hank. That was one benefit of living out of the extended stay. She was able to shower at the club and get to Nick's in Laguna Beach with little effort, flaunting her perfect figure in a sandy linen beach dress and sandals with three-inch heels. Her cheeks still had a slight glow from her workout.

She waited at the bar for Hank, and he appeared in darker jeans and a pale blue polo shirt. This shirt showed off his all American good boy looks, and she thought he was quite handsome, even though she was not entirely attracted to him. He seemed like such a good person. He was so eager to please her.

"You look beautiful as always, Maizie."

"Hi Hank," she replied with a smile.

Once again Maizie was entirely at ease with Hank. She held back nothing when he asked about her childhood. She told him how crazy her mother was, though she knew no guy wanted to hear about a girl being a victim. Hank instead seemed to become protective of her, which intensified as she let out a little about her drunk of a father, who only sometimes came home or thought to stock the house with food. She told him that she and her older brother Kip would go to a neighbor's house or walk to McDonald's with the change they scavenged from around the house in order to feed themselves. Eventually, once Kip was old enough to drive and was given a credit card, they graduated from McDonald's and ate at nicer restaurants or went to the grocery store for basics like cereal, milk, waffles, and TV dinners.

Maizie turned 16, collecting her own car and credit card, the same week that Kip left for the Naval Academy in Annapolis. She only saw him a few times since then even though they had been inseparable while they were growing up. She understood the separation only after she went away to college. She finally was able to create a life for herself that was not defined by a crazy mother in a residential psychiatric hospital, a father whose drunken outbursts colored even the most peaceful local events, or the judgment of other kids and their parents. It was easier to let go of the first 18 years by pretending they never happened. That meant divorcing her brother also.

Throughout her four years in college it had become exceedingly difficult to maintain the weekly calls at 8:00 am on Saturday with her father. She only continued because that was the requirement for him to cover her educational expenses. Even though he was barely awake and rarely sober on these calls, he was quick to correct her grammar, clarify his expectations of her, and ask her to come visit. She wasn't sure which of those topics she hated most. She'd tell him she loved him, and they would surely find a time to visit. They still hadn't, and it had been 17 years since she left home.

Maizie had never told anyone these things. What was it that made her let her guard down so much with Hank? It was quite strange. Maybe it was his honest eyes after being with her childhood friend had stirred up old thoughts. Hank reminded her of a protector, which was something only Kip had been for her in her entire life. Something about Hank made her want to just snuggle up to him and let him hold her. She had never felt this desire for companionship or affection before. It was making her feel uncomfortable. It was time to listen to him instead. She turned the tables and let him talk about his upbringing.

As she expected, Hank had grown up in an upper middle class neighborhood with a typical vanilla family. He was the middle child and only boy. His whole life he could do no wrong. He was easy-going, athletic, and kind to anyone in need. He had earned a crew scholarship to Boston College, majored in finance, and worked in biotech mergers and acquisitions with a prominent firm since the summer of his freshman year through a connection his father had made.

He was a golden boy from a golden family. However, he did not have any contact with extended family. His mother was an only child, orphaned at age 20, and his father's sister had struggled with addiction and imprisonment. Perhaps that is why his family was so close knit and focused on communication, expressing feelings, and accepting others' faults while still maintaining personally defined boundaries. Hank's father had decided it would be best to disown his extended family in order to have a healthy marriage and raise three children respectably. It was a decision his father did not regret, and Hank relayed this to Maizie in affirmation that her own choice may be for the best. At least he assured her it certainly was not uncommon and he supported her in it for what it was worth.

Hank's parents had retired to Arizona a few years ago, and two years ago he decided to move to California to be closer to them. It was his first time being away from the influence of close family. His sisters both had married and had kids in Boston, and he also had been married for a short time to a woman named Jenny. She was a beautiful and successful lawyer, and she shifted her goals from being partner at a top firm to doing part time non-profit work during their engagement so she would have more time to plan the wedding. They didn't need her salary to live well.

He said Jenny had grown tired of his family barging in when she wanted him to herself, sharing holidays between her family and his, and his long hours. He had felt like a possession rather than a husband to Jenny, and she asked for a divorce only after sleeping with his best friend and his boss. Jenny thought that the affairs would make him change. In truth he had hoped the affairs would calm her down long enough to hold her over until his parents moved. Then he'd have time for her, they could work through with the affairs, and they could start their new life together as she wanted it. Then he would consider having children.

Two months after his parents moved away, and after many sessions with a therapist, she had asked for the divorce. He had kept trying to make it work. At one point it became clear that she was going to hate him no matter what he did. It never would be enough. He finally gave up, signed the papers, and applied for a lateral transfer to Irvine. It had been a mess, he said, and a true example of why not to marry only because the checkboxes for a perfect life indicated it was time to do so.

Hank said he yearned to be in a committed relationship that would lead to marriage and children, and he admitted dating was not going well. He did not like the lifestyle most of the Southern California women expected in exchange for breathing. He wanted an educated woman who earned her own living and was in love with herself before her partner. Maizie smirked at how much that described her in most of her relationships. Only with Jared did she seem to put herself second. Interesting. She wasn't sure Hank knew what he really was asking for in a relationship with her.

Two hours passed, and Maizie and Hank both had eaten fried chicken, garlic mashed potatoes, and southern vegetable succotash. Nick's was known for its comfort food, a contrast to the bikini-clad beaches just across the street from the coast highway. They'd each had a couple drinks. He still had not tried to kiss her. And she hadn't thought about Jared. Well, at least she had not thought about Jared every second. Hank was a good distraction from Jared. She wasn't ready to sleep with him. She would run off before he could kiss her.

"Maizie, would you allow me to walk you to your car? It is dark, and though it is Laguna Beach, we do get some transients. I want to make sure you get to your car safely."

She had judged him correctly as a protector. "Yes. Thank you, Hank. You really are a quite the gentleman."

They left the restaurant and began toward her car, which she had parallel-parked three blocks away. Hank asked if she'd like to look out at the lights of Laguna Beach from his favorite perch on the way. This seemed like him testing the waters for a kiss.

"Not tonight, Hank. I really must be going. My week is nonstop starting in eight hours."

"All the more reason to take a moment for this."

"No, Hank. I want you to show it to me next time. Will you do that?"

"May I hold your hand?" he asked as he took her hand in his own larger hand. She squeezed back.

She guessed that was two yeses. He was such a gentleman, and she liked it. She was really growing to be surprised by how she felt around Hank. There was no fire in her when she thought about him. Instead she felt great about herself when she was near him. In fact she never felt better about herself than when she was around him. She was just real, calm, and confident. She felt as though she ruled all.

"I really like you, Maizie. You're an incredible woman, and you just are so beautiful. Can I see you this weekend?"

"I don't know yet. You know where to find me this week, though."

"There you go again, playing hard to get," he teased. "Can I at least have your phone number?"

"Here's my car, Hank. I enjoyed spending the evening with you. You're a wonderful man. I'll see you at the gym."

She hugged him and then pulled back a little to test where he was with plans to kiss her. He seemed tentative, so she slowly and deliberately moved her head so her lips would just barely skim his, and then moved them back and forth ever so slightly. It was a tease, and not a real kiss. It was a brush of the lips that clearly indicated she was in control, and that no more would come from the embrace. She could feel him wanting more, and also being perfectly content with the promise of more that was evident in that brushing of lips.

"Oh, God," he said.

Maizie got in her car and waved as she drove off. She could see him just standing there dumbstruck. She knew he had forgotten temporarily about her phone number. She didn't think it would matter. He was in pursuit, and she was giving him just enough to keep him there.

Still no word from Jared after three days. She remembered some sort of rule about waiting three days to call, so maybe he was just playing it cool. Damnit, she had only been away from Hank for five minutes and Jared was already taking over her mind again.

She could have taken it much further with Hank. More than anything, though, she just wanted to be alone. She wanted a still mind so she could just relax. She did not want to be thinking about Jared without knowing what he was thinking, and if he was even thinking of her. She wondered if he was out with one of the other women he said he was seeing. He must have seen a couple in the past two days. Was it one he liked for companionship or more than that?

She didn't understand how anyone could be better than she was in either aspect. She and Jared had been companions for eight years, until just before puberty set in. And Friday they had sex that surely beat what these Southern California bimbos were offering. She just had to get him in front of her again. He would melt. He would keep melting until he was completely addicted.

6 MAIZIE – SIX WEEKS AGO

Maizie was spinning out of control thinking about Jared. She didn't understand why he wasn't contacting her. Was her fake boyfriend Luke scaring him off? Was another woman going down on him at this very minute? Nothing would distract him from calling her faster than attention like that.

At work she had more conversations with him in her head than she actually had with her co-workers, and she oversaw a major project with a team of 15 people. She just didn't understand. She felt like she had to know, and at the same time she knew that she couldn't know. Instead she had to make it happen. She had to make him fall for her.

The tension was winding inside her, and it was getting to be too much for her to handle inside the dull industrial office space. It was designed for collaboration and creativity, and her best thoughts were purely inside her head to be shared with nobody. They were thoughts of having Jared want her above all. Of him adoring her and proving his love for her. Of possessing him. Of marrying him and having him forever.

She had to get out of that building. She needed to take a time out. If she couldn't be with him then she certainly could not be in this office right now. Her jaw was clenched and she could hardly breathe. She stood up from her desk and walked briskly through the large building to the side door. She had to calm down.

She crossed the office parking lot to her car, turned on the ignition, and put the air conditioning to its coldest, strongest setting. She set the alarm on her phone to alert her in 15 minutes. She focused on deep, slow breathing, and letting the tension out with each breath.

She whispered, "Breathe in..... Release.... Breathe in.... Release...." until she fell asleep. The alarm startled her, and she realized she had fallen so fast asleep there was a trail of drool running down her chin. She felt so much better. Wiping the drool on the back of her hand and smirking, she took another couple deep breaths and was ready to go back to her desk.

Turning off the car, she checked her phone and saw a message.

Jared.

'hey, i'm playing @ saloon in nb 2morrow @ 6 :) c u there?'

Her head started spinning again. She knew it. She just knew he had been playing it cool because he was crazy about her. He must have been just giving her space to break up with her imaginary boyfriend Luke.

She had to text back.

'Hi Jared, I would love to'- No, too formal.

'Hey stranger, glad to-' No, that was almost a guilt trip. He didn't need that from her.

'Jared! Cool, I'll check my schedule'- No, trying too hard to be mainstream, and mixing it with too formal.

'Jared, thanks for the invite.'- No, that was just lame.

'Thanks, Jared!'- No, that was desperate.

Maizie sighed and turned the air conditioning back on so she could concentrate on her response without sweating any more profusely than she'd begun to in the confines of the car in 98-degree weather.

Damnit, she needed another power nap. She set the alarm on the phone for 10 minutes this time. She focused on deep, slow breathing, and letting the tension out with each breath.

She whispered, "Breathe in..... Release.... Breathe in.... Release...." She couldn't fall asleep.

Damnit.

Maizie picked up her phone just as the alarm was about to ring, dismissed it, and stared at the device. What the hell was she supposed to write? She was getting very angry. Why could she speak so eloquently and effortlessly around Hank, yet barely form complete sentences around Jared? Her anger was increasing.

Why didn't Jared just call her? Why didn't he let her know he was thinking of her? Why did she think about him so much? And her only form of release was not working.

Damnit!

Damnit!

Damnit!

She smacked both hands on her steering wheel and yelled, "AAAAARRRRGGHH!"

Maizie had to concentrate on calming down. She had to focus and take a deep breath.

She whispered, "Breathe in..... Release.... Breathe in.... Release...."

40

She didn't know how much time had passed when she finally felt human again. She picked up the phone and typed a response.

'Yes.'

She hit the send button, and got out of her car. Fifty-two minutes had lapsed between receiving the message and sending her response. She had been outside for over an hour.

Heading back into the office, she felt like she had just been put through the spin cycle in a commercial washer. If she looked anything like she felt, it would be a tough afternoon. Fortunately, her beauty overpowered the beast that had just raged within. She flowed effortlessly back into the meetings and the chaos that surrounded the decisions of what content to put in which publication, and which photo shoot would take higher priority.

The newest argument was getting Dareyun Doryan to wear some new board shorts that had a hint of green when he hated green. He wanted blue, and the new signature shorts they had delivered were sea foam green in two places. He refused to wear them, even if they promised to shoot only in black and white. He didn't want to be seen in them, and he didn't want his name attached to them. Maizie's company was outraged because they'd already printed and produced the shorts with his name assigned. He wouldn't give up the design, and he wouldn't wear the green. How could they make up for the loss and promote the blue version of the shorts they'd have to get? Maizie was supposed to figure out this problem.

Did the surfers and skaters have any idea what it took to get their sports publicized? Did they understand how difficult they made it to make clothes that would sell enough to sponsor the sport and give them jobs? Did they comprehend the importance of keeping companies like hers afloat to sustain their lifestyles? She thought their ignorance must be bliss.

The 'chill', 'laid back', and 'stoner' lifestyles they aimed to emulate with their fashion were a stark contrast to the tension, bickering, and backstabbing of the public relations and media crew that got the clothing and accessories to the athletes and the coverage to the masses. It didn't really matter how she felt personally when she was down in this snake pit. No wonder the pros became so difficult to manage.

She decided to take three pair of the true blue prototype shorts and three pair of production green shorts with her to the shoot on Friday. That meant leaving for Fiji Wednesday morning. That was two days away. It was not standard protocol for her to go to all the shoots, but she did intend to get to one per month. This would be it.

She would convince Dareyun to like green. She would save the company millions, and demand a bonus to reflect that. Maizie took another deep breath, appreciating how much she loved her job. Smiling she realized it was time to leave the office and hit the gym, where she'd see Hank for the second time since their dinner two weeks ago.

The ritual of maintaining her chosen treadmill continued, and seemed so silly. Hank appeared and wiped down the machine, not saying a word and allowing her to focus on her workout. He had a sly grin on his face, and she knew he must be happy to see her after a week with his parents in Scottsdale. Arizona in the summer was not anything she wanted to imagine, nor was the smothering of his parents. They were so normal. Gross.

She was getting angry, and knew that her run today would be hard. She had been so wound up this afternoon, and this spark of anger at how normal his family was could only be tamed by a hard run. Seventy-five minutes later, she was drenched in sweat and refreshed with a runner's high. Hank appeared as she stepped down from the treadmill, and he quickly washed it. She walked away from him toward the weights, and he hurried to catch up. He was drenched in sweat also.

"I'm so glad to see you again, Maizie. May I request the pleasure of your company at dinner tomorrow night?"

"Welcome back, Hank. It's another busy week for me. I have plans tomorrow, and I'm leaving the country Wednesday morning."

"Would you join me for a quick bite after we work out?"

She didn't like how he phrased that, as if they were working out together. It was too quaint, and her anger was again hinting at the surface. She was so anxious about waiting 24 hours to see Jared. Now that he finally had asked her on a date it was too much to have to wait for the next day.

"Hank, it's your lucky day," she said with a big smile. "And I'm done with my workout."

"Nick's in an hour?" he asked.

Maizie realized she had a great opportunity at that moment to surprise Hank. They were both dripping in sweat. She wanted to implant an idea in his mind, so she remained silent for a moment. She knew he would continue following her as she walked toward the locker rooms, and she could sneak him into the small hidden corridor that housed the drinking fountain. As she approached the corridor she spun swiftly and stood with her back against the wall so he would face her naturally when he turned. She was ready, on her tiptoes, lips parted.

Hank was confused when his lips suddenly were pressed to Maizie's. He didn't even know what happened. They were in a corridor. He was kissing her. She was kissing him back. He moved his sweaty body closer to hers, engulfed in the hot kiss, and felt her sweat mixing with his in the hot embrace.

Oh my God, he had her pinned against the wall. Was he dreaming? He pressed himself harder onto her body. He'd waited so long to have a kiss with this woman, and he had never been more aware of how irresistible she was. He grabbed her arms and pinned them over her head, as he pressed closer. He kissed her hungrily for what could have been seconds or minutes. He didn't know or care.

As suddenly and mysteriously as it had begun, the kiss was over. He was stunned, and also exhilarated. They were so sweaty. She was so hot. He had no idea what had come over him. He'd never kissed a girl in public. How had he suddenly kissed this amazing woman? He wanted more.

"Yes," Maizie said as she moved out of the corridor and into the locker room.

She knew it would take him a moment to process that he had best hurry to get to Nick's in an hour for dinner.

She knew that he'd be preoccupied at dinner thinking about their sweat-drenched kiss. He would be imagining working up to a sweat together without their clothes. The best part was he thought he had been the one to initiate the kiss.

At Nick's she knew exactly where his mind was the entire time. The power she had felt around him previously was elevated even more over this second dinner. She could have repeated, "Blub, blub, blub, blah, blub" for two hours and it wouldn't have mattered. He had only one thing on his mind: sex with her.

She wanted Jared to look at her like this.

Maizie decided to make a mess of her dessert on her chin to see if Hank would notice. He didn't. When she started to wipe the whipped cream from her face with her napkin, she paused and caught his eyes. Putting down her napkin she let him reach out and assist her with his lips. They both chuckled, him nervously and her luxuriantly. She knew he was imagining licking whip cream off more than just her chin.

She loved planting sexual fantasies in Hank's mind. It was such fertile ground. She wanted to keep playing with him, so she said she had to go and asked if he'd show her the spot he'd mentioned last time they were at Nick's. Tonight would be a perfect night to take in the beauty of the Laguna lights by night. Naturally, he agreed.

When they got there she stared purposefully out at the blackness and breathed in the fresh, salty air. She glanced away from him at the lights that ascended from the black edge of the water up the mountain. They were in this tiny sphere of the world, held inside Laguna Beach by the ocean and a mountain. Nothing else mattered, and here she was supreme. With Hank, she was the only thing in existence.

Hank stood next to Maizie and put his arm around her. This was one of those times when he felt most connected to her. Her depth was evident as she absorbed how special Laguna Beach was, and he was happy to be sharing this special spot with her. He hadn't stopped thinking of how he'd kissed her earlier. She had kissed him back. He desperately wanted more.

He let his hand rest along the small of her back with his fingers reaching toward her side. She felt amazing. She shivered the slightest bit, so he repositioned himself to stand directly behind her. He wrapped his arms around her front, pressed his body to hers and rested his chin on her head.

The contact was too much. He immediately was aroused, and he was afraid she'd feel it and get upset. He felt so creepy taking her out here with an erection. He didn't want to be that guy. He simply wanted to kiss her. He took a step back, pulling her with him and then sneaking between her and the rail. As he had done earlier that night, he suddenly was kissing her as they spun around.

He did not want to offend her with his erection. With him against the rail it would be up to her to lean in. He kissed her tenderly, and she responded passionately. He teased her by nibbling on her lower lip. He was imagining being inside her. He was pushed over the edge by her teasing her tongue slowly across his lips, and he smelled a sweet, musty scent as she moved to kiss his neck and nibble her ear.

Now he could pull her tightly to him and not worry about offending her. He wanted her so badly. He was afraid he wanted her too badly. He'd never been so aroused in his entire life. He was completely powerless over this woman. He kissed her hungrily until they weren't kissing anymore.

"Let me walk you to your car," he said.

Maizie let Hank walk her to the car. He definitely was turned on by her without much touch, and he had gotten lost in her kisses. He was such a great distraction from Jared.

"Thank you for a wonderful night, Hank!"

"Maizie, when will I see you again?" he asked nearly breathlessly.

"I'll be back next week. See you at the gym."

She got in her car and drove off before he could say more. She knew it was cold. She just did not want to give him her number, and she knew he was about to ask.

Tuesday evening, Maizie had everything she needed for the trip to Fiji ready and in her car. She planned to go right from Jared's to the gym to the airport on Wednesday. Since she had booked last minute, the only flight with a first class seat available was departing at 11:30 am.

She arrived at the saloon in Newport Beach at 6:20 pm and was hit with the stench of an old bar in which every surface had been saturated with liquor and vomit multiple times. This was hardly a classy place. The patrons consisted of fishermen, drunk tourists, and a few surfers who probably had dropped out of college or never started.

She was one of three women in the bar, and it looked like the other two were Jared's groupies. Was she the only one of the now five or six women he was dating to know that he was dating other women? She assumed he had sent each of them the same message yesterday and took a gamble on who would show up. The crowd was diverse enough that it wouldn't be obvious to someone who didn't know better. This would be interesting to see how he worked the room when the band took breaks between their sets.

One of the groupies was seated at a table of men, one of whom was paying attention to her and refilling her beer from a plastic pitcher while trying to keep her interested in what he was saying. She occasionally touched his arm and nodded, but mostly she was staring blatantly at Jared with a dumb smile on her simple face. Groupie two was sitting alone in a booth across the room. She looked uncomfortable, like she was waiting for something or someone. However, she too was staring at Jared with a dumb smile on her simple face.

Maizie decided her game would be easy. She would not play one. She simply would go to the bar and order a scotch on the rocks with a glass of soda.

The bartender took her order and introduced himself as Sonny. He was well into his 70s, or at least he appeared to be with his crusty, rugged physique, raspy voice, and air of wisdom. Back in his day, Maizie was sure he had been quite handsome and that he would be an entertaining man to engage in conversation.

"Does this band play here a lot?"

"Depends what you mean by a lot, young lady. They are here every Sunday and Tuesday. Why, does one of them tickle your fancy?"

Maizie was entertained by the old man's vocabulary. Did he have any idea what Sick Suck meant?

"I went to grade school with one of those guys. It's just funny to see him on stage. I never had thought of him as a rock star."

"Young lady, we got no rock stars here. Case you haven't noticed, place is hardly full of music connoisseurs, if ya' catch my drift. Hell, most o' these guys don't even realize we got music. They just come for a drink. Band, though, they bring in young blood like you. Tryin' a turn this place around 'n sell. Need more business for that. Your friend's band can keep playin' long as they want. Bringin' in more people. Young people. Christ, in my day this was the place to be. The ladies were foxy. The men were dapper. Oh, yes, it was quite different in those days. That's why I bought the place. Now I just want out. I'm 68 years old. Clock's a tickin'."

"What's your favorite type of music, Sonny?"

"Well, believe it or not young lady, I used to play with some big names when I was a boy. Headed to Julliard I was. I like the classic string instruments, like the bass and violin. That's real music."

"I love the symphony, and I believe you. Your eyes lit up talking about it."

"Free o' charge."

Sonny smiled and walked away, and Maizie found herself alone with two free drinks in front of her. As if on cue, the music stopped and Jared approached her. Maizie was smug that he was coming to her first. It showed her that she was the one he wanted to see most. She was number one on the list.

"You guys sound great!"

No reason to say anything about the last time they'd spent together or how she had snuck out. No need to ask if he had been thinking of her. She was in front of him because he invited her to be here. She was the first person he approached when he got off the stage for a break. Nothing else mattered. He hugged her.

"Hey, yeah, this is like the greatest place to play since we can like totally just try out whatever we want and like nobody really cares. So we just, like, jam, you know."

"It sounds like you are having a lot of fun."

"Yeah."

She had forgotten what it was like to pull the words out of his mouth and had to concentrate on doing so or risk looking like one of the other simple-minded floozies. Gosh, did they have something coming if they even for a second thought Jared could be theirs. She admired his physique and gave a mischievous smile. He picked up on the sexual energy she was putting out and put his arm around her back, leaning into her.

"So, like, I have to like say hi to some people, you know? Are you going to like hang out for a bit? I want to see you later."

Score.

"Oh, I can stay for a while. How long do you play?"

"Sweet. We're like on until like nine or so. It's like really good to see you, Maizie. You like look really hot."

Score again.

She smiled and planted a soft kiss on his lips briefly. It was a perfect balance of showing affection while not getting too intimate. She thought he either would be nervous the others would see them, or he would want to respond without hesitation. Either way, he did not get to choose since she pulled away so quickly. He blushed. She smiled at her ability to tease him.

"I'll like see you at the next break, Maizie."

Maizie grew rather bored of listening to Jared's band play. He was slightly entertaining to observe as he attempted to navigate the room with grace under the eyes of his groupies. It seemed he wanted them there to please Sonny and also to boost his own ego. The woman from the music festival, who had cornered him on the stage like a cat, had arrived at 8:40. She may have grown bored of the band earlier, for which Maizie actually admired her strategy.

Regardless it was Maizie who was going home with Jared tonight. Not the cat lady, and not the other two simple-minded bimbos. In fact, she would seal the deal with ease. She had noticed Jared peeking at his phone almost like clockwork every 15 minutes. She pulled out her phone.

'Jared, would love to hang out after you play. Leaving for Fiji tomorrow, so otherwise would be a while.'

She hit send. God, she loved her job.

With a couple scattered exchanges with Sonny as the only other thing keeping her awake, she was quite happy when they were done playing at nine. She saw him look at the phone, and he smiled at her with a lopsided grin. He looked like he'd been slipped a drug and was not fully capable of comprehending what he had in store because it was so much better than anything in his current reality. Yet he would have to work to get there.

Score again.

When they finally played their last song, the cat lady again went to the stage and positioned herself as she had last time. Well, she certainly was an assuming and possessive feline who already had lost the fight. She just didn't know it. Maizie wondered how many times this cat woman had been passed over by Jared, and if that is why she had taken to setting herself firm on the stage to separate Jared from her competition.

Did Jared even notice? She was certain he did on some level and just chose not to be boxed in by it. He didn't seem like the kind of guy who would let the cat woman stand in the way of what he wanted. He was aloof and casual enough that it would not reflect poorly on him to be a ditz and ignore the cat woman's signals if what he wanted was something other than the cat woman.

Maizie was curious to see how Jared would handle this. She did not have to wait long. Jared jumped down from the stage and gave the cat woman a distant hug. She could tell that the cat woman knew the stage move had failed. Jared moved off to another table to bid goodnight to the only other remaining simple-minded female fan, whom he walked to the front door kindly and gave a gentle, distant hug.

He was actually rather good at this, Maizie thought. He definitely knew how to keep his options open without the women dropping him. They wanted to compete for him. He didn't have to compete for them, which seemed ideal for a laid-back surfing musician. It didn't look like they had anything going or any real connection. Maybe he had made up the other women to make her jealous. She was certain that anywhere he played it was only the last half hour that he needed to acknowledge the woman he took home that night. She noted all these observations and filed them away for later use.

Sonny must have known immediately to whom she was referring, so she thought, when she'd ordered her first drink. Maizie signaled Sonny to get a beer for Jared and another shot of scotch to top off her remaining rocks. Jared had returned to the cat woman and engaged in a playful conversation. He cut it short and walked her to the back door, where he lit the cigarette she'd put to her lips.

Gross.

He gave her a longer hug and kiss on the cheek before returning to assist in dismantling the band's equipment. The other members mostly had been talking to the surfers and locals, not having graduated to the level of attracting dedicated groupies.

The cat woman had disappeared into the night, and she and Maizie had not made eye contact that night. She wondered if the cat woman had even seen her sitting at the bar. It didn't matter. The cat woman had lost. She could go home and lick her wounds before returning Sunday as she surely would.

Maizie nursed her drink as she waited for Jared to pack up his gear. He'd glanced up at her several times and indicated it would be just another moment, ensuring she wouldn't leave without him. She signaled that she had bought him a drink and would be at the bar with her own, which Sonny topped off once again.

As much as she was glad to have won Jared's attention for the balance of the night, Maizie was beginning to grow truly bored. This was not something she would want to endure. She didn't care for music especially, and his band was not an exception. She liked looking at him, and also wanted it to be over a lot sooner so he could tend to her.

He would have to stop playing. It really was that simple. He didn't have much talent anyway. In order to be with her he would either have to truly focus on honing his skills to become a professional musician of rock star caliber, or he would have to find another hobby that did not bring these simple women to admire him in dive bars. Perhaps he could surf more, or take up woodworking. He could take up gardening. There was plenty of room on his property to start a garden. Then he could cook for her, too. That would keep him busy and contained.

She knew to approach this matter with Jared carefully if she wanted to keep him. Slowly and gently he would think it was his idea to take up the home-based hobbies. She was in direct alignment with his parents on his need to move on from his dreams of being a casual musician. She wanted him to stay out of bars and keep close to home so she knew where he was at all times. He would be happy. Her boyfriends always were perfectly pleased with the new lifestyles she chose for them. It was so much less stress for everyone.

Finally, Jared bid farewell to his band, came over to the bar and toasted his beer, which by now was sweating onto the cocktail napkin from having waited so long. Maizie gave him a huge smile, sincere with her vision for his future happiness.

Jared was glad to be next to Maizie again. When she smiled at him, all he knew to do was plant a kiss on her hot lips. He was ready to take her back to his house and continue what they'd started last time. He couldn't get her there fast enough. He swallowed down his beer in two gulps, and asked Maizie for the keys so he could drive them to his place. He wanted her now. Her smile was making him crazy.

As soon as they arrived at his house, Jared pressed his mouth on her and struggled to undress Maizie while dragging them both up the stairs toward his king size bed. He didn't care about taking her clothes off slowly and looking at every bit of her. He had done that already. He could do it again later. He just wanted her. Now.

He was harder than he'd ever been and ready. She was attacking him with similar hunger, and her legs were wrapped tightly around him. He could barely remain standing and hold on to her. He almost tripped over the sandals she had flung off her feet and up the steps. It took every ounce of effort in his being to concentrate on getting himself and Maizie up the stairs where he wanted them to be. He didn't know if he would make it.

He managed to unbutton her jeans by the time they reached the landing halfway up the stairs. He stopped on the landing and turned to set her down so she was lying on the next set of steps. He pulled her jeans and lacy panties quickly down over her feet and flung them over the bannister. Since his face was passing by her crotch, he teased her lightly with his tongue and pulled her legs wide apart.

On his knees, he was able to get his jeans and boxers down to his knees with one hand. He could feel her hands grabbing fistfuls of his hair as he used the index finger of his free hand to push inside her. She was wet and ready.

He pulled his face away and moved up to kiss her as he pushed himself inside. He was thrusting with a hunger he felt coming from the depths of his manhood. She was calling out his name, and he thrust harder. He grabbed onto her hair with one hand, gripping it firmly in his hand.

Oh, yeah. He just kept going. She was calling his name. He was crying out to God.

The next thing he knew he was waking up from a slumped over position on the landing. Holy shit. Was she gone again? What time was it?

Maizie was on the plane to Fiji hoping that she was not bruised too badly from the rough exchange with Jared the night before. It had not been great, and he seemed to have saved all performing capabilities for what to him may have seemed like a porn quality screw session on the steps and what to her was incredibly uncomfortable.

Her job at the photo shoot would require her to look hot, and long bruises across her back from the steps at Jared's were far from the ideal accessory for a couple days on the beach. She resigned to the fact she may need a cover-up, and employed her deep breathing and nap sessions again to calm down.

Jared would need a lot of training. And the musician gig had to stop. As adorable as he was, and as special as he had been to her as her first crush and best friend in the tough first year of middle school, there was not much he was offering at his current stage. If things didn't look up in the next date or so, she would have no choice but to quit wasting time with him. She was not interested in a pet project.

There were plenty of men who could offer her financial security, luxurious gifts, and something of a challenge. She already owned Jared sexually, and even then she had to be in front of him for him to act. The man had no ambition, and he may not even pursue her until after he had lost all of his manliness. At that point he would not be interesting anymore. She knew she did not want to spend her nights with his music.

What to do with Jared.... She had yet to even have a conversation with the man. And that was just it. He was a man-child. He may have aged physically and become incredibly handsome. He lived to fulfill a childlike fantasy of being a rock star, and it seemed he had regressed in mental aptitude. Every third word was with 'like' or 'you know' or another casual slaying of even the most basically structured sentences. How dumb was he?

7 DELORES – TWO WEEKS AGO

Delores couldn't remember the last time she had laughed so heartily or enjoyed so much to be in the company of a man, much less a true Southern gentleman like Chandler. She was impressed that he had paid attention to the details of who she was, and that just from their correspondence behind the cloak of the dating service he had picked up on her preferences for outdoor dining. He had gone beyond making a reservation for the clubhouse and made plans that would remove the typical distractions or potential sightings.

They had shared a wonderful private picnic on the green at the club. As a cardiologist, Chandler admitted he was well aware of the dangers of common menu items such as bacon and beef, and he only indulged occasionally in these animal-laden cravings. His preferred style of eating was similar to Delores's so he appreciated the macrobiotic menu, prepared at his request, which may have scared off a simpler man.

Chandler made Delores laugh. She made him laugh in return. At several points the laughter produced tears in two sets of eyes and echoed through their bellies and hearts. They had been so engrossed in conversation that they lost track of time and Chandler's departure time to return to Tennessee. When Delores noticed the heat of the sun had shifted to her left side as she looked out over the green and onto the ocean, she jumped in her Adirondack seat.

"Chandler, you must go or you will miss your flight!"

"I am just cherishing this moment with you. I have not felt so lighthearted and content in some time."

Delores smiled. "I can relate entirely. This is so natural. You strike me as such a wonderful man."

"Listen, I know this is new. It just feels like the door has opened to something very special. I do not want to imagine that being concealed again, and I am afraid of missing out on your life over the next three weeks. Why don't you join me in Tennessee later this week? I would love to show you around on my turf before my next trip to California. Would you think about it?"

Delores was both surprised and excited by this request. She wanted it to continue. She was excited to be connecting to her companion so quickly.

"Yes, I'll look over my appointments for the week and consider it. Perhaps I can make it a working trip. Now you had best be on your way. Otherwise you will get stuck on the redeye flight, and tomorrow will be painful."

"Okay. I know this may be silly, but here is my card. Call me tonight. I want to hear your voice before I go to sleep. We can discuss your travel plans for later this week."

Delores accepted the card from Chandler and tucked it carefully inside her camel suede clutch. He stood and took her hand to assist her up, if for courtesy rather than support. Standing face to face they wrapped their arms around each other in an embrace that grounded the connection they had built over the two-hour lunch conversation.

"Go! Run!"

He kissed her cheek and dashed off up the hill that rose around the clubhouse. Just before he disappeared out of her sight, he turned back and waved with a sincere smile on his face. Seconds later Pedro made his way down around the bend to ensure Delores was escorted properly to her car, which he had pulled around, started, and cooled with air conditioning to be ready when her meal had concluded.

Climbing into her metallic Tesla and beginning the route to her father's care facility, she felt lighter than she had in months. She thought that Chandler understood her without digging into the minute details. He did not inquire about her personal or family wealth, the status of her country club memberships, or the specifics of the corporation she had formed while an undergraduate at Harvard when the typical internship route proved too shallow for her aspirations. She did not need to regurgitate her resume or detail her dating history either.

She did not need to discuss the tragedies that led to her father's slow and certain demise from highly functional to residential care. Since he had medical background, Chandler had taken it at face value when Delores mentioned her only family was her father. She told him she had placed her father in a residential care facility the previous year so that he could have the constant medical attention and daily routine that would allow him to live the remainder of his life as happily as possible.

Mostly the pair had laughed about the trials and tribulations of traveling to foreign countries, learning languages on the spot, and developing coping mechanisms. For a change, she just got to be Delores. Once again it was enough simply to laugh. She felt like a child again in a world in which anything was possible.

Free of responsibility, pain, or drive, she allowed herself simply to feel and remain happy.

This was something to which she wanted to grow accustomed again. Where had that gone? When was the last time she had felt so free? Driving along the coast highway, Delores pondered this question seriously. It really had been a while.

Her father was in a slightly dark mood when Delores arrived. It amazed her how even a half hour shift in the schedule they had set up for her visits could throw off his response to her. He did not know who she was, yet he was acutely aware that someone who was to appear at 2 pm had not. He did not expect someone at 2:30. It pained her to think of missing several days, and she wondered what that would do to his routine. She knew that each moment spent with him was to be cherished.

Juergen always had been such a strong and generous man, however demanding he had been of those around him. There was nothing he asked of others that he had not done himself at some point, and that had made him an outstanding mentor. Delores knew the man with whom she now shared tea was only the confused shell of that strong man who had been a cornerstone to every part of her life.

Delores also knew she needed to pay attention to herself and her own life so she would not sink into a deep depression. She had not realized she was entering such a state until lunch with Chandler. The lightness she felt with him, and that still lingered a couple hours later, was a stark contrast to the fear of loss that had enveloped her since she had moved to the Newport Coast home.

It was clear that her father's condition was getting worse. She knew she had to take small steps to get back to her regular life, or at least a life that was not defined by the 2 pm visits, in order to keep her bearings when her father passed. Chandler was one part of the equation. Delores smiled as she thought of him.

She glanced across the table at her father in his matching wingback chair. Juergen's eyes were closed. Those beautiful hazel eyes into which she had looked with wonder so many times in her life no longer held the answers. It was up to her. While they shared the same physical space, the forty years they'd shared as father and daughter lived on only in each of their minds. Delores would cherish them forever. Her father may have been past the point of accessing them ever again.

Perhaps Wendy was right. This may be the first time she would actually have room to welcome another man to play a significant role in her life. Was this Chandler?

When Delores arrived home, she took some time to play fetch with Ferdi and Polly. As German hunting dogs, this pair was glad to have a job. They would fetch their tennis balls regardless if they saw where the ball went. They could smell for it. Delores admired the intelligence of the pair and their graceful beauty as they ran across the lawn. Their lives were so simple. She was reminded of herself as a child.

Delores pulled out Chandler's card and dialed his cell phone from her blocked home number.

"Hello, Chandler. I hope you had a fine journey home. I really did enjoy meeting you this afternoon and appreciate how creative you were in making it a special time. I will call you later this week about my arrangements for travel to Nashville. I'm certain we will find a suitable window to spend more time together this week. Good night. I'm thinking of you and smiling at the thought of being with you soon."

Delores would have her assistant, Chloe, find a suitable cause in Nashville for her to investigate with a visit this week. The rest of the time she could invest in allowing this relationship to unfold.

This was a major turning point in her relationships. She had dated several men long distance. It typically was an easy way to ensure, subconsciously of course, that she would be separated by more than physical distance. None had ever been too serious.

Most of the men with whom she had relationships had been married. That was another way she had kept them from getting too close or from posing any threat to her father's status as the top man in her life. Another man held her heart and their lives belonged to another woman. That situation always had delivered what she wanted so conveniently. The demands were simple and mostly focused on when and where they were meeting. There was always the occasional getaway for a weekend or longer.

These men, almost without fail, were happy to spend time with a beautiful woman who had no expectations of them like those they otherwise faced constantly from their wives, mothers, children, and associates. She imagined it was not unlike her escape with Chandler that afternoon. It was an excuse to enjoy being alive, accepting of faults and strengths, and allowing another person to treasure all of that.

There was no need to lie with the married men. She never wanted to break up any homes. She never entered the relationships thinking he would change his mind and leave his wife or family for her. Quite the contrary, she liked the fact the relationships would not grow complicated. Being the other woman allowed her to have her own life outside the demands of a full time partner. She did not have to compromise to meet the needs of a family, which she experienced through them and to which she was not attracted.

She never thought she was stealing from the wives. If anything, she was ensuring the marriages stuck together by refreshing the men, encouraging them to spend time with their children, and listening to what it was that really bothered them without any judgment or selfish agenda.

She wanted the company of these successful men with no strings attached. When either had their fill, the arrangement simply faded and there were no hard feelings on either side. Often these men remained in her life as business contacts. There were no friends or possessions to separate, no lawyers to consult, and no children to console. It had worked for many years.

On one occasion Wendy had inquired about one of her beaus, asking, "You seem to be having a wonderful time with this one. Is it serious?"

"Oh, Wendy, it can't be serious. He is married," she had replied with a chuckle.

Only now, entering the dating scene again as her father faded, did she consider the option of a deeper commitment. Of course there still was the matter of explaining to Chandler her true identity. Making up the name Glenda now seemed like a silly move. It was the signature of reduced commitment. She had not taken the matching service seriously.

Monday morning Chloe was able to locate three organizations in Nashville for Delores to visit and evaluate on her trip to visit Chandler. This would be her first time back in the field since she had moved to her father's home in Newport Coast, and she knew it was another important part of re-establishing a presence in her own life. Chloe arranged for the shared private jet to be reserved to carry Delores from John Wayne Airport on Wednesday and return on Sunday.

Delores would stay in a suite at the Hermitage, the only suitable hotel in Nashville. She loved that it reflected the taste and aura of former President Andrew Jackson. It was stately and elegant, yet welcoming and cozy at the same time. Chloe also arranged for a car and driver to be available at any hour over the duration of the stay. Delores had never rented a car, and driving in the new city was not worth the effort. Chloe knew exactly what arrangements to make and which car company to contact.

Delores admired Chloe and often wondered what drove the young lady to be so attentive. She was grateful for the efficiency and effectiveness demonstrated at every task. She did not know much about Chloe. She did remember that Chloe was freshly returning to the workforce after having her first child when she'd been hired. Delores had traveled so frequently during Chloe's first months at the Beverly Hills office, and then suddenly shifted to working remotely to accommodate her father's needs. As a result Delores and Chloe had very little personal interaction.

The two worked like a seasoned pair, though, as Chloe not only seemed capable of predicting what Delores would do next but also would have prepared for that scenario. She knew Chloe had met her husband through an online matching service. She was tempted to step outside protocol and tell Chloe what the real purpose of her visit was, and assumed Chloe probably already knew.

Monday evening Delores called Chandler again, choosing a time she was certain he would be unavailable.

"Chandler, it's me. I'll join you in Nashville from Wednesday until Sunday. I am counting down the days!"

After she hung up, Delores wondered if she was taking too much control too early in the courtship. He didn't have her number because she had not told him her real name, and she did not want to change her voicemail greeting. She had essentially removed his ability to court her except through the service's messaging service, which seemed so impersonal. Still, he could send a simple message to her and regain control.

He had not messaged to say he had returned home safely, nor had he contacted her regarding her own travels to Nashville. She had to go. She had to confess her identity in person before it was too late. Not wanting to explain her silliness over the phone, as that certainly would be taken as an insincere gesture to make right a matter that had been a lie prior to their introduction, Delores continued to climb deeper into her false identity.

On Tuesday evening she had yet to receive a message from Chandler. She wondered if he had been sincere when extending his invitation. Surely he was at the time. Was it a spontaneous offer, or did he seriously want to ensure he did not miss a moment of the life he had begun to see on Sunday? Delores wished she had given him another way to reach her so he could have taken the initiative. She was tempted to log in and send him a note to tell him she would be there and to please let her know what his schedule was, and also considered such a message may be too forward. She hoped that he was okay. She hadn't heard of any planes crashing, and there had been no fatal car accidents reported from Sunday.

It was odd. She never had experienced this doubt and questioning with any of the married men. With them it was simple, and a system always was worked out so as not to arouse suspicion and to ensure no evidence was left. Delores did not know how to proceed in this case with her new single suitor, and decided to do nothing.

She went shopping and prepared for the business side of the trip. Regardless what happened with the man, her career could be revived. She would get back out in the field and grow her business. Delores was flying to Nashville on Wednesday, and she would make the most of whatever was meant to happen.

8 MAIZIE – FOUR WEEKS AGO

Maizie was on fire. When she was hot, she was hot. The trip to Fiji for the photo shoot turned out to be one of the greatest experiences of her career. Dareyun was convinced quickly to love sea foam green, and she had turned out to be something of a muse to the incredibly sexy young surfer. She had hung out with him and his friends for nearly a week to get the best shots, and she was able to participate from the wave. Pulling on the life vest was an ideal way to hide the ridiculous inch-wide bruises that ran across her back in three spots. Riding the jet ski she got more bruises, and these served as battle scars to show off back on shore.

She directed the photographers to get closer, to go faster, to capture crazy angles, and to shoot longer sequences than ever before. After the first day's photos were shown, she inspired Dareyun to try new combos that they could cover exclusively for the shorts. Everyone was inspired by her charisma and relentless pursuit to capture the raw talent of the young surfer. He had forgotten entirely about his sea foam green shorts. It was all about his surfing, and that was a beautiful thing.

With such enthusiasm evident in this professional surfer, she wanted to take the lifestyle shots even further. With her special bag of unassigned clothing, she pulled out some items that could be featured on him, his friends, and their girlfriends as part of the full suite of surf style. One of the lifestyle photographers had been directly on her wavelength in terms of creating the special, intimate feel she wanted to capture. Since he was an island boy and surfer himself, and having lost a limb to a shark, he had a degree of respect that could not be earned by anyone else in the industry.

He and Maizie were able to elevate this particular campaign to the greatest of her company's history. They captured the most extreme moves in waves over 20 feet and paired it with bonfires, friends, and happiness that would invite any reader to feel part of the inner circle. People would spend money to have the inner circle feeling. It was magical. Her focus was spectacular.

When she came back to the extended stay suites, she knew she had to graduate to the next level fast. She finally secured a rental in Laguna Beach. She had been able to justify a large bonus when she returned from the journey to Fiji. Without her, the company would have lost a full season of production for a design it had hoped to feature, and possibly would have ended the sponsor relationship with the young Dareyun. As she left it, Dareyun and his friends were electrified by their rekindled passion for surfing, and the one-legged photographer would hop at the chance to collaborate with her on another masterpiece.

The CEO had recognized that her contribution was invaluable, and he rewarded her with a bonus that was so large she considered looking for a different, more luxurious place than the one she'd secured via email in Fiji. That thought passed quickly. She was done with the extended suites. The place she found was perfect, though small, and it would allow her the flexibility to move up to a place she loved more when she became familiar with the area. Searching from the hideous Lake Forest hotel was no longer bearable.

Maizie was certain her new apartment was not in Hank's neighborhood, though if she ran into him that would be fine. She had not seen him since her return and assumed that he would be there very soon to wipe down her treadmill. He served little purpose otherwise, and had no means of contacting her.

Jared, on the other, hand, had become somewhat obsessive in his efforts to contact her. He became borderline possessive, even. Once she returned to California and was reconnected to her cellular phone provider, no fewer than 20 messages popped up from him. This was a surprising turnaround from the casual, passive man who had missed his chance by a couple weeks.

'Maizie, where did u go?'

'u r so hot'

'Maizie, when are u cuming back?'

'playing @ saloon 2nite @ 6. c u there?'

'miss u'

'can i c u soon?'

'maizie?'

'what's up?'

'where r u?'

'where did u go?'

'hope 2 c u @ saloon sunday @ 6'

'thinking maybe u wanna b on top next time?'

Gross. That was the last thing she wanted to think about. He was the equivalent of a 12 year old mentally, at best. There was nothing sexually appealing about that. He was not a rock star. He was not a porn star. In fact he lacked talent to consider either, yet was delusional enough that he probably believed he could be both. He had proven he was entirely out of touch with his audience and with his mate in that single Tuesday, and took it several steps beyond plain proof in the series of text messages.

What ever happened to calling someone? There had been no conversation, and it seemed wanting him was a mistake. He would have to figure it out himself because she was too busy to tell him otherwise. He was history.

Now that she had moved into her own place by the beach, where she had planned to be months earlier, it was time for some new candidates. No more man-child idiots like Jared. She wanted a man of substance. Four years of moving around taught her one thing: being the new girl had a fine window, and she would capitalize on that once again.

With her new stories from Fiji, being on fire at work, and living in her dream apartment, Maizie was sure that the online dating site would deliver some matches that could complement her life well. She wanted a man with money, purpose, and drive who would admire her, cherish her, and treat her to luxuries greater than $25 burritos at Javier's. Her sights were set much higher now.

Logging into her profile, Maizie put her marketing and media skills to quick use with new photos from Fiji. She had been beautiful in the existing photos, and the new ones from Fiji made her irresistible. Any man in his right mind would be drawn to her sparkling eyes, and the shimmer of her skin that gave a realistic depth to her perfect curves as captured on camera. She came to life in the photos, and from experience she knew the viewer would imagine the sensation of touching her since the photos were so vivid. God, she loved her job.

With the new photos in place it was time to set up her introduction and all the other information her matches would be able to see. She knew exactly how to market to an audience that consisted essentially of men like Jared or who wanted to be like Dareyun. Her pictures spoke to any man. The words had to match the sexiness and elevate her to a respectable level as well. Any man she wanted would be interested in someone with an above average IQ.

She again fell back on the advice of her drunken father, who had broken it down simply to her in one of his life lessons lectures. She had to be careful to be soft, yet tough; interesting, yet not overshadowing; successful, yet not bossy or domineering. He had taught her to identify the traits that would undoubtedly be discovered and deemed negative, and exploit them from a positive perspective immediately.

After an hour Maizie felt confident that she had put the right material on her profile, and it was time to select preferences for her potential matches before finally setting the geographical preference to match California. She had purposely left it set to the East Coast until she had the appropriate marketing set. She did not want to open it up to California matches that didn't meet her criteria, nor did she want to have appropriate matches see the long list of changes she was making. That seemed weird to her.

It was important to her that a consistent front was presented. She needed to be perceived as a mature, together, and dependable lady. The final thing to do was fine-tune the preferences for her matches. Then she could submit her new zip code and confirm the search for her new matches.

She decided that her matches should be older, so they would have had the opportunity to achieve true success and learn some lessons along the way. They should be old enough to be done with the bar and club scene. No liberals. She had no interest in a bleeding heart whose attention would be focused on helping others in a way that ensured they'd always need more help and attention.

No, the match had to be successful and respectable. He definitely had to make at least $150,000. In this area that was nothing. It was not even a down payment on a one-bedroom cottage in her neighborhood, where there was no such thing as a house below $2,000,000. She wouldn't consider a man whose lifestyle did not match or exceed her own. Drinking was flexible. It was acceptable if he drank a few times a week at most. A daily drinker sounded sloppy and lazy.

The only nationality she would consider was the same as her own. Somehow, with interracial relationships having grown in her generation, she knew that some men would put down white if they actually were only 25% white. That was as far as she could imagine straying. Her mother was crazy and could be crude, but one of the things she had said about a neighbor had always stuck out to Maizie: "What was she thinking when she went out with that brown fellow? Didn't she realize she might end up with little brown children? Just look at them!" Maizie wanted to eliminate the possibility of little brown children. She didn't know if she wanted children at all, and if she did have them they certainly would not be of the little brown variety.

With preferences set she put in her Laguna Beach zip code and indicated being open to matches located within the smallest possible radius, which was 30 miles. This was far greater than her preferred range. It was the best the service could do. The ocean being directly alongside her eliminated at least half the circle. She pressed 'Apply Settings' and went to the gym to exert herself on the treadmill while the service set to work.

Since it was later than normal, she was not surprised when Hank did not show up to wipe down her machine. It was time to find a trainer now that she had settled into Laguna Beach. She didn't want to be limited to the treadmill at this cheap temporary place that was the standard of the middle class. That idea suddenly was repulsive.

When Maizie returned home and powered on her computer, she was delighted to have five matches presented. She looked through their profiles one at a time.

Stuart from Newport Coast, 47
Vice President of Global Non-Profit
My most favorite thing to do in the world is to give to others, for, my passion is compassion, and for me, that is showing others their value. Whether that is challenging them, causing them laugh, showing them the simple pleasures in life or turning their pessimism and fear into workable FUN solutions. Most find it really difficult not to have fun, smile, or be inspired when around me. This is my gift and I share it demonstratively in every aspect of my life.

Okay, this was exactly the kind of guy she was not interested in meeting. He was out to prove something by helping as many other people as he could. That just seemed bizarre to her since the people he was giving to otherwise had nothing to offer in return. What a loser. On his quest for self-promoting through others, he definitely would have no time for her. And what kind of superior prick thought he had all the answers to other people's problems? That would be a guy who could only look at other people's problems, not admitting he had any of his own. She blocked this fool.

Ralph from San Juan Capistrano, 45
Independent Film Producer
I believe that adults have it all wrong and could use a reminder from the younger version of themselves - openly pursuing new adventures and experiences (FUN) with the willingness to listen and consider others perspectives. This, at the most elementary level, is learning and growing... and life needn't be so hard. Also, although I understand the importance of status, as it pertains to climing the social ladder and driven by acquisition, I prefer to collet expereinces rather than things and listen to people instead of pushing my opinionated position. I very much enjoy people if that still is not apparent.

Ralph also seemed a bit full of himself, and he was the second match in a row who put 'FUN' in his bio. He sounded like he would be 'fun' to talk to over a meal. He could be teased and intoxicated by flirtation, but he would be turned on only by himself. He may have money, or he, like Jared, may simply be a man-child hoping to breeze through life stating his dream rather than actually working to make that dream a reality. If he had money it probably was not earned through work.

No, she was betting he was a man-child. On the off chance he was not, she decided to keep this match open. He would see that she had viewed his profile if he looked at that part of the dashboard on the service site. If he pursued her, that would be a start. She had the distinct impression that men did not pursue with the same vigor in California that they did in other places she had lived.

Bradley from Laguna Beach, 44
Business owner
I love art, nature and health. Art because I love when a painting or piece of music stirs an emotion in me. Nature because it is more beautiful than anything created by humans. And health because it helps me see the beauty inside me and around me.

Hmmm. Maizie had heard about 'canyon people', a distinct group of artists that lived in the canyon just inland from Laguna Beach even though the hippie movement had taken place decades ago. To own a business, he must be an art dealer or something similar. Maybe he sells vitamins. In the photos, he looked too worn for someone who was so natural and in touch with art, nature, and health. She could picture him dancing around in an Indian or Tibetan costume and humming for himself and for customers. She thought this guy either must be one of these 'canyon people' as he seemed to be commune-like or on some really heavy anti-depressants. Either way, she felt uncomfortable meeting him or communicating. For all she cared, he could continue his peaceful, flowing life away from her. That would be better for both of them.

Philip from Newport Beach, 47
Finance Director
On a quite often basis I like to go out to eat, grab a drink with friends, practice yoga, watch a movie, go walk around somewhere interesting, or fiddle around my place. If all else fails I like to lye on my couch and play on my computer while watching TV or blasting music :) My occasional leisure time activities include the likes of travel, concerts, snowboarding, weekend road trips, or exploring something new.

Philip had a strange writing style, and Maizie wondered if maybe he was foreign. He seemed like a slightly more grown up version of Jared, complete with a career in finance. He was honest about what he did outside of work, and it was evident that he needed entertainment from multiple sources in order to survive. This, too, was fertile ground for a man who needed to be instructed how to live. A woman had to tell him what he wanted or he may be in great danger of running out of things to do in search of himself. She sent this quirky fellow a smile. He may be fun to devour one day as puppeteer.

Michael from Anaheim, 42
I believe that nice things are worth waiting for ...

Michael would be waiting a while. Seriously, if that was the best he could do, he had better accept that the wait might extend the rest of his life. Block.

With such a low quality of matches, Maizie realized that she, too, might be waiting for quite some time.

9 DELORES – ELEVEN DAYS AGO

Delores had the driver bring her to the plane at the civil time of 9 am on Wednesday. She was escorted on board the 10-passenger Learjet, her luggage was stowed, and they started to taxi to the runway. It was so simple to fly this way. She truly could not imagine dealing with all the chaos of a commercial flight. What a waste of time!

It had been a while since she'd flown. In an effort to cut costs and appear less extravagant in an era that suddenly and aggressively despised wealth, she had been persuaded to sell her beloved custom Boeing 717 and buy into a partnership with four other corporations for this smaller aircraft. It had been good timing to cut back on expenses. Only months later, she had moved from her Wilshire penthouse to Newport Coast and dedicated herself mostly to the care of her father. It felt good to get back into the mobile mindset.

Delores realized this style of travel was still new to her. This was yet another step in reclaiming herself. Her entire life she had flown on larger private aircraft, and the simplicity of the 10-passenger Learjet was comforting. It was more her size, in all honesty. She wasn't as comfortable moving around this cabin as she had been in her 717 as she felt the need to watch her head. However, the cabin design proved to be clever in delivering all the functionality to which she had been accustomed without requiring movement from one area to another. She was able to choose a seat and request for the attendant to change configurations whenever she needed.

Today's flight was short - a mere four hours - and the attendant was a young gay man named Chee-yong. At least, she hoped he was gay. He assured her he would take wonderful care of her needs throughout. Lucky for him, her needs were minimal. She would drink an herbal medley tea forty minutes after takeoff, and Chee-yong would serve her a summer spinach salad with grape tomatoes, pea sprouts, cold wild rice, braised broccolini, and a four-ounce salmon steak au pauvre in a light caper vinaigrette dressing.

Timing meals on short flights was a delicate matter. It had to be served within two hours of the start of the flight so she would be able to transition to the Eastern Standard Time, a three-hour shift from the time in California. It had to be a late lunch since she had just finished her breakfast at eight. If she ate much later, though, then her evening meal would be postponed beyond a reasonable hour. Chloe always took great care to ensure her meals were coordinated properly with time zones, and Delores appreciated just how quickly Chloe recalled the details of her travel requirements. It had been a while since Chloe had performed such tasks.

Delores looked out the window, pressing her face to it lightly, as the small aircraft gained speed and took off at a sharp angle over the Pacific Ocean. The plane maneuvered smoothly, and it felt like she was floating through the sky on a magic carpet. Looking down, she recognized the small area that had been her world for the past couple years only because she knew she was flying over it.

Her world had become unrecognizable, like a question mark, and she barely recognized herself in it. This trip really would do her good. Her corporation had been running itself for the last five years in more of a sustaining mode. She had not expanded or enhanced anything since before Nora died.

Delores chuckled at the thought of sweet Nora, continually asking her, "Now what is it that you do again, dear?"

Before Delores could answer, Nora would say, "Oh, yes, you have that global corporation that would go out and train people about donating money to charities all over the world, and now you just stay in Beverly Hills."

Her father's fourth widow had been right about the fact that her corporation used to be more active in expanding its clientele, investigating the legal and financial validity of the claims of many non-profits before allocating her clients' funds to them. As an heiress to a sizable fortune that had compounded and grown through the point of her first access to it on her 18th birthday, Delores had been a prime target. Many organizations claiming to be charities had wanted to take her money in exchange for nothing other than her humiliation.

Juergen had trained her well to respect her money, and Delores had placed her fortune into a charitable foundation that only would donate to reputable entities. She was so skilled at analyzing these charitable entities that she had formed a corporation to validate the claims of charities worldwide.

Delores never had to be played for a fool because of Juergen's training. She had made a couple of mistakes over the course of her career, and felt that those were made early enough to recuperate fully and add texture to her otherwise flawless presentation when asked. She had enough wisdom from these experiences that she did not have to repeat these mistakes.

Most of her clients had become satisfied selecting from her existing list of charities, formed over a span of 15 years since the start of her career. Somewhere along the way she had lost her passion for exploring and uncovering the real intentions of the charities, whether good or bad. It had become too depressing for her to travel to third world countries to discover imaginary charities that benefitted fat middle-aged white men and not the children they claimed to be saving. It was easier for her to live in her penthouse on Wilshire Boulevard and travel only to maintain relationships with existing clients and charities.

She sent her younger associate, Joshua, to investigate a few charities, and he did a satisfactory job. Joshua had come to her directly from the Peace Corps, and he was a gem. He was able to clean up and wear a suit like he'd been born to model for the cover of GQ or Esquire. On the same day, he could slip into jungle garments and hiking boots and sleep on dirt. He enjoyed both for different reasons. Over the last two years, it was Joshua flying on the Learjet to maintain the relationships.

Ruth hadn't meant harm nor had she been insinuating that Delores was lazy, yet it seemed if Delores had been more active Ruth would have remembered the activities of the corporation. Ruth instead would have asked where Delores had gone most recently or what her newest investigation had uncovered. Those were the questions she had asked when they had met initially.

Today, for the first time in nearly five years, Delores was engaging in the expansion of her client base, and she would emphasize the importance of spreading the wealth to new markets. Her list had grown stale, and she wanted to run a great corporation again rather than waste away in complacency for another single day. Oddly, it seemed this was something that would have pleased Ruth as well.

If Ruth was happy, Juergen was happy. If Delores was happy, Juergen was happy. Now Delores was content because she was fulfilling her own dream and longtime mission. This would make these two dear people happy to see if they were able to.

Chee-yong interrupted Delores, who had remained in the same position staring out the window since the plane was on the runway. She realized she had been daydreaming for 40 minutes, assuming Chee-yong adhered to the schedule for tea delivery. She requested he retrieve her briefcase, and she pulled out her iPad to look over the prospectus files

Chloe had prepared about the three groups in Nashville.

Bunny Fitzhibbons ran the first group, and it appeared to be newer money that Bunny wanted to put into the medical industry in India. Bunny's mother had gotten arthroscopic surgery in Nashville that was orchestrated by a doctor remotely in India. Bunny wanted this technology to be available to people from all walks of life. Delores had a few other ideas to make this a more worthwhile investment with greater distribution of benefits. Bunny would have to be open to a radically different mindset, and Chloe surely would have devised a more personal profile had more notice been available.

This was one Delores would have to go into blind and pull on her early skills to build a relationship from the ground up to gain the trust of this woman. The meeting with Bunny would be at a country club just outside Nashville in an area that once had been famous for horse plantations. Now it was a coveted area for new money that wanted to rub elbows with the more established families of Nashville. Delores was rather certain Bunny came from the latter circle.

Dolly Jones was a retired teacher who wanted to help provide AIDS medications to children in Africa. It appeared Dolly had lost her daughter to AIDS several years ago, and her daughter had acquired the disease giving medical attention to a child in Africa. Delores assessed this as a simple enough goal, and she had several contacts from which to choose in order to find the charity that would make best use of treating younger people living with AIDS. Delores wanted to include some domestic beneficiaries in this, and hoped that Dolly would be open to diversifying her funds. She would remind Dolly that the purpose of such charitable giving is to put money to use in a way that humanity could benefit to the greatest extent possible. Inner city children in Nashville deserved a portion of the improvement in society the benefactor wished to bestow. They would have breakfast Thursday morning at the Hermitage Hotel where Delores was staying.

Finally, Birdie Collins was on the board of a privately held company whose growing profit margin demanded an improved corporate responsibility program. The company specialized in contamination control products for industrial settings, and the shareholders wanted to shift their tax burden immediately. They wanted a diverse distribution plan that would benefit pulmonary, ophthalmology, and dermatology diseases. Their meeting was set for lunch Friday at 1:00 at the Hermitage Hotel.

Chee-yong again appeared and pulled Delores out of her intent focus. She had not yet completed reviewing the file, though there was plenty of time to do so before Friday. The meal Chee-yong placed before Delores was beautiful. He bowed silently after presenting her lunch, and disappeared from view as quickly as he had appeared. He was good.

The Learjet descended and landed gracefully in Nashville exactly on schedule, and a car was waiting to deliver Delores to the Hermitage. After checking in and taking a tour of the suite, Delores decided to pull out her laptop and check her emails and messages on the matching portal. No work items required her personal attention. The afternoon nurse from her father's residential care facility sent an update, as she promised to do daily. This message informed Delores that Juergen's condition was unchanged.

Still, there was no message in her matching portal inbox from Chandler. How odd. It showed he had not been active since last week. This was such a spontaneous excursion for her. Now that she was here, he simply must call. Delores was tempted to pick up her cell phone and call Chandler. She did not want to give the hotel number in case he called when she was out. She would give him her number so when he did call, she would be able to answer, or at least access the voicemail immediately. That meant she had to change her voicemail. There was no other option.

Before she finished dialing his number, she reconsidered. Taking a deep breath, she realized she was about to make herself far too available to this man, who had done nothing more than send a few messages through an internet dating service, meet her for lunch, and invite her to Nashville this week. He had disappeared after lunch and had not responded at all to her.

Instead of making a desperate fool of herself, Delores decided to call Wendy and fill her in on the last two weeks' worth of internet dating. Wendy would assure her that all would be well. Wendy could be counted on to lay blame, throw a "pity party" and move on to the next action quickly.

True to her reputation for reliability, Wendy answered on the second ring.

"Oh, Wendy! Do you have a moment? I sure have created a fine mess with that online dating racket you roped me into!"

Wendy laughed. "Delores, I'm sure it isn't as bad as you think. What's going on, dear? I have a few minutes to talk before I leave to pick up the twins from tennis camp."

"For starters, I'm in Nashville to see a man I met for lunch on Sunday. He invited me here, and I haven't heard from him since I made the arrangements to fly out."

"Delores, back up, honey. You are WHERE?! What? Start from the beginning, sweetie."

"Okay. A few weeks ago I decided to look at my matches on that service. There was a nice cardiologist splitting his time between San Diego and Nashville, and we messaged each other for several days before arranging a lunch date. The date was wonderful. He arranged a private picnic on the green at Pelican Hill, and it was so light and energizing. Then he invited me to join him for a few days in Nashville this week since he wouldn't be in San Diego for a while."

"So you just flew to Nashville? After one lunch date? How did that work? Does he know your real name?"

"I didn't tell him. I forgot during lunch. He doesn't have my number, so he wouldn't get my voicemail to hear my real name. I wanted to tell him in person, and it seemed like a good time to get away from Newport Coast. Wendy, my life there was heading for a deep depression that I want to avoid. I just don't want to be alone waiting for Daddy to die. I need to get back out and live. I realized that after lunch with Chandler, and I had to take a chance. I left him messages that I would be coming out to Nashville today through Sunday, and he simply has disappeared. I just arrived to my hotel, and I'm not sure what to do."

"Sweetie, I know this is a tough time for you. You know I always tease you about being Daddy's girl. Your father is an incredible man, and I know he was all you had to support you through your life. But you cannot go looking to fill that void with the first man who comes along. You are a treasure. It is not your job to be leaving messages and arranging travel. If he doesn't even acknowledge your call, then this Chandler is not worth your time. He's obviously not ready for you. And you have gone ahead and thrown yourself out there for him to take or leave. Honey, he needs the opportunity to miss you."

"I am just so used to being with married men, where the deal is on the table from day one. Even with that variety it has been over a year since I was active with a man. Wendy, what is my next step with Chandler?"

"How can you be such a brilliant business woman and still be such an adolescent with men?"

Delores chuckled as a tear came to her eye. She was overcome with embarrassment for how silly she had behaved with Chandler. This was a game she did not know how to play.

"Honey, you send that man a message and say that something came up that will keep you in California after all. It's that simple. Either turn around now or take some time in Nashville. Use that vacation to feed you. Do whatever you like. Just don't do it with him in mind! Do it for Delores! You don't want to be messing around with San Diego or Nashville, anyway. See, after one date he was already done commuting to you! Don't sell yourself short, Delores. You are not a charity case. You need to be pursued. I have to run to get the kids. Goodbye, angel."

"Thank you, Wendy. I love you."

"I love, you, too, sweetie."

Delores decided to order room service and have a bath drawn. She would stay in Nashville and feed herself with the new professional prospects Chloe had found for her. Perhaps that was the reason Chandler was put in front of her in the larger scheme of things. Other surprises had been greater than this. Chandler may just be a catalyst. After ordering her meal, she sent a message to Chandler through her company's secure office proxy in Beverly Hills so that it would not be traced to Nashville.

'Hello, Chandler. Something has come up that will keep me from meeting you this week in Nashville after all. I feel badly to back out, yet I must.'

She did not sign it. There was no need to lie outright by signing it 'Glenda'. It was difficult enough to use the proxy. Hitting send, Delores did not like the feeling of dishonesty that came over her. The proxy was a lie. She could justify it in many ways, the simplest of which being that it was her proxy and she was on a business trip. It still didn't sit well with her.

This was worse than using a false name because it was intentionally deceitful. In all honesty, the name change was as well. But she had forgotten about the name change when she actually was on the date with him, and it didn't come up in their messaging beforehand. If Chandler had been the kind of man to call others by their first names in conversation, then it would have been resolved much sooner.

No, the name really did have purpose. Delores had plenty that had to be protected and withheld prior to entering a relationship with a man. Her business and background were concealed for good reason. This was self-defense and preservation.

What had come up this week was herself. Wendy helped nail home self-respect. Now it just had to last through the week. Having sent the message and processed the layers of lies that already created imbalance in the foundation of the relationship, Delores was glad to be staying in and enjoying space to herself outside of her home. She did not have such solid footing in her life now, and she was trying to let go of her old life so she could define the next portion of it.

Two days in Nashville had been like a dream. Delores enjoyed the mixture of old southern hospitality, the manners and respect exhibited by the men as a standard rather than the exception they were in California, and the depth of the community history. The community's history was so rich compared to that of Newport Coast. Several families had remained prominent in Nashville since settling over a century ago. Families who still would tell of how things had changed with the Civil War held property. Plantations were a way of life for centuries, and only the way the labor relations ran had changed.

Delores was reminded that this was a place where things were produced, and where music had been able to reach the ears of the masses. Even black musicians had thrived for decades in this southern region that had clung to slavery. The culture was beautiful and fascinating.

By Friday morning, Delores was feeling like she had when she started the corporation. She was energized and impassioned at the thought of making charitable donations to those who would use them honestly and properly. The first two clients had been true "Southern Belles", regardless of being over 50 years old. When Delores had proposed the diversification ideas, each lady was receptive. Delores now had the task ahead of her to research and validate recipients of the funds.

Her first two days had been surreal, as she stepped into a life that had been on hold for so long. Friday at 12:50 pm, Delores took the elevator down to the lobby. She enjoyed the high ceilings and rich, solid details of the Hermitage Hotel lobby and lounge. Again it was a sense of the roots of her country that she missed in Newport Coast. Her meeting with Birdie Collins was for lunch at Capital Grille, the hotel's flagship restaurant, and Delores wanted to do some mental preparation before entering.

Long ago, Delores had adopted the technique of taking up more space, even if this was only the mental image in her mind, so that she would use all of her power in a meeting. There were so many women who sat small, crossed their arms and legs, and did not bring their influence with them to the table. Yet so many men would lean back, cross their arms behind them, spread their legs, and fill the room. The unprepared female would shrink as others took up all the space.

Delores imagined herself filling up the room. In a wingback chair of the lobby, she stretched her arms gracefully overhead, imagining that they reached all the way up to the chandeliers and through the stained glass in the ceiling. This lobby was perfect for her warm-up. It appeared to any passersby that she simply was stretching lightly. It was tasteful. If they thought anything else, it was none of her business. She continued her routine for five minutes and felt fully prepared to meet Birdie Collins, though she had not revisited the file since Chee-yong had brought her lunch two days prior.

She had requested the Hermitage staff notify her when Birdie arrived, and at one o'clock sharp a host came to the lobby to escort her to the lunch table. Delores spotted Birdie at a table in the corner beside a large antique-finish black and white image that was to imitate both a photo and the view out a window of a centuries' old United States Capitol building. Delores again admired the history that she was presented on her visit to Nashville, and exuded quite a natural smile as she walked through the Capital Grille dining room. She felt regal.

Birdie Collins stood when Delores reached the table, and the two women smiled politely and shook hands. The host held out their chairs in turn so the women could be seated. Birdie was a plump and voluptuous woman, though not distinctly obese. Her body had curves that she accentuated with a floor length maxi dress. The magenta fabric was uplifting, and a silk scarf with bright orange, yellow, and blue flowers in a finger-paint style brought out more energy from Birdie. Her jewelry was large and gold, typical of the South, and the diamonds on her wedding ring must have totaled over seven carats. The shade of Birdie's nail polish was bright magenta, and colorful bangle bracelets adorned her arms. Birdie's hair was a chestnut brown streaked with red, and it was difficult to tell what her natural hair color would be. Her makeup was bright and overstated as well. Everything about Birdie Collins screamed out to be noticed by everyone who laid eyes on her.

Quite to the contrary, Delores was simple and elegant in her exquisite Armani suit of a natural sand-colored wool, stark white silk shell, and sand-colored pumps with small white buckle at the toe. Her hair was pulled back in a gentle bun with not a single strand out of place. Her earrings, necklace, and tennis bracelet were platinum with diamonds, and she wore a plain ring on the ring finger of her left hand. Her makeup was always minimal, with just enough blush to accentuate her cheekbones with a healthy glow. Her lipstick was subtle, which allowed the detail of her eyes to pop out with subtle and minimal yet effective eye shadow techniques.

The women were the same age and shared a passion. They wanted to fund a cause that Birdie's corporation could back proudly. Delores doubted there was any common ground other than this business interest. Her neutral clothing and calm demeanor typically allowed her to find a way to become relatable to anyone quickly, and for a relationship to ensue naturally from there. Birdie was something else and may as well have been an alien from the first impression. Delores never had sat across the table from such a woman, and she had no idea what was going to unfold. She wished she had read more of the prospectus Chloe had assembled. If she spoke Delores was certain it would sound fake and ruin the meeting with the first sentence. She was also certain that Birdie would speak quickly.

"Well, I am just so happy that your office called me on Monday. I was going to be traveling on this darn trip down to New Orleans to meet with a lawyer down there so he could give me some advice, and it was just all going to take so much time and effort. The timing was wonderful. My husband, you see, he had been out of town for a while, and I really wanted to be around to see him this week. He will be joining us for coffee after lunch. I wanted to make up my mind, and then have him come in so he feels a part of it. That's the trouble with marrying a man who doesn't understand what it's like to come from money. From the looks of you and the pretty little ring on your finger, I'm sure you have run into the same thing. Having more money than him, it is like I always have to reassure him it is his money, too. Though really it isn't, if you catch my drift. End of the day, we all know it is up to me. I just want to keep my man feeling like a man. So I let him participate. Really, whatever he says, well, it doesn't matter. The decision is mine. I want you to know that. Also, bear in mind that when I make a decision, it is a final decision and that there is no way I will change what I want. Unless of course I decide I want something else. So tell me, Delores, what do you have in mind for my funds?"

Delores realized she had underestimated the intelligence of her companion based on her appearance. Birdie was sharp, observant, and outspoken. She did business like a shrewd man, and within two minutes of meeting had rushed past all the things that would have come out on the golf course over several hours.

Still, Delores wanted to keep her own personal details to herself. Birdie reminded her of a professional poker player, who was able to manipulate others with expressions and divulging information at specific points. Delores was well trained to keep the relationship focused on business. She was glad she had gone through her personal space expansion routine prior, and imagined herself stretching out to the Capitol building. She was vast and powerful, and though understated she would not be plowed by the likes of Birdie.

"My pleasure entirely. There are thousands of people who will benefit from your corporate responsibility program. It really is an investment in humanity. I have a few ideas for pulmonary, ophthalmology, and dermatology. First, I'd like to understand the vision you hold as the board member entrusted with planning it. You obviously have a respected opinion, and I'd love if you would tell me more."

Over lunch, Delores and Birdie were able to agree on the direction that Delores would take in selecting the charities and causes that would receive the money. Though they were such opposites, there were certain moments when they did chuckle at similarities. Both had specific instructions for the preparation of their food. Birdie wanted melted butter and bleu cheese to top her large steak. Delores wanted her salmon poached with no salt, oil, butter, or dairy in any of her food.

Each woman stated her order with absolute certainty and left the poor waiter terrified to get anything wrong with either. He was not accustomed to such a powerful, estrogen-rich table, and these two had thrown him for more than one loop. At first he had suspected they were secret shoppers. He wanted to get a perfect score. He was a professional, after all, and the Grille needed to know how lucky they were to have him.

They were so demanding. If he messed up he was afraid he would get fired, or worse, get the lousy sections. He did his best, and when that wasn't good enough he did better. When a man approached the table, the waiter breathed a sigh of relief that the estrogen level would be cut.

Birdie was looking over Delores's shoulder, and for the first time had diverted her attention directly away from the table.

"Here he comes. My handsome husband. Darling, meet Delores. Her company has been selected to manage our new corporate responsibility program."

Delores turned to her left, where Birdie's gaze had rested, and found herself looking directly at none other than Chandler.

Chandler did a double take as well.

Glenda?

Chandler Collins?

She had only looked at his card the two times, and had not even thought to associate him as anyone's husband, much less the husband of her new client Birdie Collins. Of course he had disappeared this week! There was no way he would be able to manage an affair with Birdie around. The phrase, "a little bird told me" correlated directly to the eyes and ears this woman had, and she easily had a flock of birds telling her everything.

"Chandler," he said with his hand held out.

How shocked did they look? Delores pretended to have no recollection of this man as she took his hand coolly and shook it.

"Well, hello. I just had the most enjoyable conversation with your generous wife. She has spoken so highly of you. I am glad you were available to meet us this afternoon, given your busy schedule as a surgeon."

Stop talking. Stop talking now or it will be obvious to Birdie that something is going on. Stop.

"Excuse my surprise. I was expecting a stuffy old man from Louisiana. The pleasure is all mine."

He quickly shook Delores's hand, and then leaned over to give Birdie a hug and kiss, placing emphasis on the duration.

He whispered, "Hello, my love," and tickled Birdie lightly.

Delores felt a wave of nausea rush through her.

Chandler took a seat between the two women.

The nausea increased.

Birdie chuckled and said, "That's my Chandler, always wanting to have fun. Now back to business. Delores here founded her company while she was at Harvard. Before she could even drink I reckon. There really is nobody more seasoned than her. Chandler, I think she can do us proud. Delores, come on, spill the beans."

With Chandler around, Birdie was even more gregarious. It was as if every knob in the woman's body turned from loud to blaring. It already was challenging to handle her on her previous volume, and Delores was having a difficult time maintaining composure.

She felt sick.

She remembered stretching to the Capitol building.

She could do this.

She was doing this.

She looked at Chandler and began explaining the details of her plan and the potential recipients, thankful to fall back on discussing a subject she knew so well, explaining the benefits and potential pitfalls of several key details.

"That sounds solid enough to my ears, and I don't need to hear anymore. I trust you've explained it all to Birdie already, so no need to go through again." He smiled, and turned to Birdie, "Honey pie, you have done a wonderful job. The board will be thrilled to hear the plan. You have outdone yourself."

He put his hand on Birdie's leg and squeezed by her knee. She smiled, and he blew her a kiss.

Delores felt dizzy for a second, and pulled herself together quickly.

After 15 grueling minutes of small talk, again more similar to what typically would be discussed on the golf course, Birdie made it evident through a series of rustling movement that she was preparing to leave.

"Now, Chandler, I want to you talk about the medical details with Delores so you can make sure she knows what she is talking about, you hear? We already signed on a big exclusive contract, and I want you to help me with the details, Chandler. Understand?" Chandler stood to pull back Birdie's chair, and the couple embraced as she stood.

"Delores, we will talk soon. Now you can have this all set up for me in two weeks you say?"

"My assistant will have the paperwork in your hands within two weeks for your review. We can take it from there. It was a pleasure to meet you today, Birdie, and I'm certain we will change countless lives with your contributions."

She stood and shook Birdie's hand, calling on all of her strength not to faint or vomit.

Chandler excused himself to walk Birdie to the door. Delores took a deep breath. What had just happened? This was an ominous position. She feared what would happen to her reputation if Birdie even suspected there was a connection between her and Chandler.

This was bad. No, this was a disaster. Delores took another deep breath, closed her eyes, and opened them to see Chandler settling into his seat next to Delores.

"Chandler, what just happened? You're married?"

"Maybe I should be asking you, GLENDA, what is going on. How did you find my wife? Are you stalking me? What in the hell is going on?"

"Me? Stalking you?"

"Yes. Here you are in Nashville sitting across the table from my wife. How did you find her? What in the name of the Lord are you doing talking to my wife about her board's money?"

"This is just surreal. I didn't know you were married. I had no idea that was your wife. I... I... ahhhhh. This is..."

"Who are you anyway? You are the lady I met on Sunday, and you also are not at all that lady. What are you doing with my wife?" He was clearly agitated.

"Chandler, please calm down. We cannot afford to make a scene. We are going to have a civil conversation. I suspect your wife has eyes and ears everywhere. Now I understand why you were not in contact this week. Civil conversation. Okay?"

Chandler was still agitated. Delores was as cool as could be on the outside, once again taking advantage of her space-filling routine and calm nature.

"Look, I had a wonderful time with you on Sunday. I called you as you'd requested, and decided I may as well take a risk and come to Nashville. I told you about my father, and after lunch Sunday I realized it was time for me to get back into my life. I decided I would come here, and I had hoped it would be a romantic excursion to the South. I needed to believe in a fairy tale, if only for a few days."

"How did you get my wife involved in all this? What do you want with her? How did you find her?"

"I had no idea you were married until you walked in 20 minutes ago. This is so embarrassing. I wanted to have something to do while in town. I don't have any clients in Nashville, so my assistant lined up three appointments with prospective new clients. This last one was with your wife. I had no idea. I never would have come here if I had known."

"Are you being honest right now? You obviously know my wife has money. You are not trying to blackmail me or anything now, are you?"

"Me? No! Chandler, I was so embarrassed when I FLEW OUT HERE without even a confirmation message from you. You asked me to come to Nashville, and I took the invitation seriously. Here I was on Wednesday, over a thousand miles from home, sitting in a hotel suite, and I realized I didn't even have a date! I felt like I'd been far too desperate."

Delores looked at him. She looked him square in the eyes.

"You still don't even have my telephone number! I wanted to tell you in person that my name is Delores, not Glenda. It was too desperate to call, so I decided to go ahead with my work. I sent you a note to say something had come up that prevented me from getting together this week."

Delores looked at him with open, honest eyes.

"I left it up to you to send me a message. The biggest surprise of my career came when, on my third appointment in Nashville, I end up meeting you again through your wife."

Delores shook her head.

"Excuse me, Chandler. I am having difficulty digesting all of this. Will you explain yourself, please?"

"Oh, dear Lord, Delores. Look, I really like you. I didn't expect that. I went to lunch just to have a pleasant conversation with a beautiful woman.

I wanted to tell you in person that I was married. Look, I swear to the Lord that I wanted to have you to Nashville and tell you in person that I am a married man. Dear Lord, I don't know how to do this!"

Chandler's gaze was direct into Delores's eyes, and he was calmer. She believed him.

"I deceived you in my profile, and you did the same to me. So we are even on that. Over lunch Sunday it was too nice a time to get down to the truth of things. Again, we are even on that. It sounds like we both have a lot to protect. Am I right?"

Delores nodded.

Chandler had regained composure.

"Birdie told me she changed her plans because my assistant had set up this appointment with her. Imagine that!"

Delores laughed nervously at how ironic it was. She wondered if he really would have been truthful without the surprise meeting.

"I understand you would not have much space to get in touch with anyone else as long as you are in the same town as her."

"You really nailed that assessment. She is more than a little overbearing. And I am very clear on the fact that I am not leaving my wife. You see that I cannot. She would ruin me, and it would destroy her. Lord knows she would take you down in the process, too. Anything good that was to come of any of us meeting, of anything we could accomplish together, would end up meaning nothing and only bringing destruction. I cannot live with that. I don't want that to happen."

"Chandler, what do you want?"

"I want to know you. I want a life outside my marriage. The worst thing I can imagine is to miss out on knowing you."

"You don't know me."

"I know enough about you to know I want to know more. You are a gorgeous creature."

"I am not sure I want to know more of you, Chandler. I did not go to lunch with you to be a sideshow. I want a partner with whom I can grow and share my full self any time, and not just when it is convenient with our careers and my partner's separate family life. I want more than that. What if I want my own family? You just said you are not leaving your wife. How would you give me what I want?"

"Right now I cannot. Right now is not forever, though."

"Do you and Birdie have children?"

"We have twin girls and a boy on either side. The youngest is 10."

"What if I wanted my own children? How could you give me that?"

"We can work out something. Really, it doesn't have to be so difficult does it?"

"I will not have a man with two families. That's absurd. Have you ever done this? Have you ever actually had an affair?"

"No. It's always just been lunch. Please, consider meeting me for lunch next time I come to San Diego. You have my word I will not try anything other to be wonderful company for you. Being with you means something in any capacity. Will you consider it?"

"How dare you!" Delores got up from her seat and walked away. She crossed the lobby and was at the same grouping of chairs in which she had sat before this odd meeting with Birdie when Chandler caught up with her. Chandler walked swiftly ahead of her and turned around to block her from moving further through the lobby.

"Wait, wait! I apologize. That was going too far. Please, sit. Let's not make a scene, as you said before."

Chandler seemed to be scared, and the color had drained from his face.

Delores was compelled to sit and finish the conversation. She wanted closure, and realized that may require more information. She was still overwhelmed by the situation.

"Look, neither one of us is innocent here. I truly apologize if I have hurt you. I wanted to tell you in person. Sunday just was so enjoyable I did not want to ruin it. It still is not ruined, regardless what your name is or what you do for a living. That is not what makes you special to me. You are a remarkable woman. Some man will be very lucky to catch you."

Delores remained silent.

"You won't be rid of me so easily regardless. Birdie has decided to go with you for her board's new program."

"Chandler, you and I can only ever see each other by chance or if Birdie arranges it. Do you understand that?"

Chandler looked at her without speaking for a moment. She returned his gaze and did not blink.

"Yes. I respect that your business relationship takes precedence over seeing a married man. I understand it would be best for everyone if I step out of this and leave any future meetings to chance. I do not like it one bit. I wish things were different."

"I wish the fairy tale hadn't come crashing down so suddenly. I had looked forward to knowing you, Chandler. Somehow there is a better plan here of which we are a part yet we are not yet aware."

Chandler nodded.

"This puts me in a terrible compromise," she said.

Delores saw that this conversation still was stirring up a lot of emotions in him.

"I can turn her down."

"I wouldn't advise that. She has made up her mind that she wants you to work with her. That's it."

Delores realized Chandler was begging. He sincerely wanted to cover his attempt at adultery. Would he deal with others as practiced in such affairs as she, who would know how to keep their cool? If he were exposed, would she ever be exposed? Would it be fine to do business with Birdie, given that Chandler would have to stay to the side?

He did not get to walk away from this. She did not know if she would be able to walk away from this either. She had to make him suffer now so that many people would not suffer later. If he did not contain himself, then she could come crashing down as well. At this moment in time, all the power was in her hands. Her decision would affect many people, and Juergen had taught her how to deal with such scenarios in a humane fashion, easing the burden of the responsibility inherent in her occupation.

"I do not like entering this relationship with Birdie knowing what I do about your intentions, Chandler. There is more at stake than hurt feelings."

"Please, just continue with Birdie. That is all I am asking. I promise not to contact you. We shared one meal, and it was wonderful. You did nothing to harm Birdie. I promise I will not ask you to. I don't know what I was thinking before. Please."

She knew if she treated people well on a consistent basis, they eventually would trust that the treatment would continue. They would learn how to relate to her on a clean foundation. Or they naturally would be removed from her life if that were beyond their desires. Sometimes changing was too much for someone, regardless of the gain. Occasionally, they would be back after another experience or wisdom gained over time indicated the relationship with her was one worth fighting to maintain. No matter what, Delores retained control of her behavior, and she was able to know without doubt that it was nothing she had done that had soured a relationship. Only time would tell what Chandler's personal constitution contained.

"Chandler, I do not know who you are. I do not trust you. I want to be very direct with that. Tell me why I should not just walk away from your wife professionally. You are not ready to walk away from her personally. Why should I stay with her?"

"Please, just don't hate me for this. Don't make a decision now that will harm others forever. Don't. She is innocent, and she really wants to feel good about something that she has done good and right. She wants to create a legacy." Chandler stopped talking and shook his head, gazing down.

Delores remained silent, allowing him to process whatever was going through his mind. She genuinely wanted to hear his side and have more information on which to base her decision. He was terrified of Birdie.

"You know, the legacy I was talking about in my profile was the very one she wants to create. She is a good person, Birdie is. Believe me, she has done nothing wrong and deserves the opportunity follow through with this. I have been really jealous and selfish. I have to let her be Birdie and be successful. It hasn't come easy to her or to me to succeed, and she just seems to be so much better at it. Seems I have just about messed that up for her. I guess I didn't realize how stupid I was being. It's more than just me involved here."

"Chandler, you have put me in a difficult position. I will think about whether it would be ethical for me to continue into this contract with Birdie. You will know directly from her. Let's be perfectly clear here that you will not contact me regardless of my decision. Your indiscretion has put others in jeopardy. Most women would lose it in my position. You should know from experience that there is nothing worse than a woman scorned. Do you realize what you are asking of me to continue in this deal? Do you have any idea- any at all- what is at stake? I have built my company on honesty and in the name of honesty and integrity. How does this reflect on me?"

"Delores, please listen to me. We all have surrendered a part of our lives for another person. I know you understand. You are going through this with your father right now. Sometimes that means more than anything in the world, and others it begs the question of what we are doing, what we want, and even who we are. I know you understand. I am just asking that you surrender to what you know is right for Birdie and the possibilities of her legacy. I get to surrender to her, and our kids, too. You have done her no harm, and I swear to you I will turn around and support my wife. Like I am right now. She deserves this chance. It will mean something."

Delores thought it ironic that she had sat in this very place two hours before and felt certain she was the most powerful being in the room. Now she felt that even though she could make her decision and stand by it, there were forces on all sides opposing a positive outcome. She could walk away, and that may be best for her. That would be the best for her company on the surface.

If Birdie ever suspected anything it may be worse, though. Birdie may dig and exploit regardless if she did business with her. Not taking the contract may be far worse, in fact, for it would show that Delores was more interested in an affair than in that which her company claimed to do. She may be more true to Birdie by continuing with the contract.

The decision of integrity was quite difficult to determine. Turning down Birdie would raise deep suspicion, and having left on perfectly amicable terms, the change may be blamed on her husband. This was not good. There was no clear answer.

"Oh, goodness. Whether I walk away or stay with her, we will not be cleared from last week for quite some time. I fear this being exposed for either of us. I will delete you from my account with the service so I never show up on your profile. It was under another name, anyway. The payment information should remain private. I placed two calls from restricted lines to your cell phone, so you had best delete those messages anyway. I just have to calculate these risks. Look, the very saving grace of this may be this ring."

Delores pointed to the narrow band on her ring finger. It was simple. There were no diamonds or embellishments. It was a plain stainless steel band her father had worn on his working pinky finger, and that she now wore on her ring finger because it was the only one on which it fit.

"Birdie may have assumed I am married."

Chandler cocked his head, more questions rising to his mind. Again, he was becoming emotionally charged.

"Good Lord, Delores, what is this now? Are you married? Who are you, really?"

He looked like he was about to melt into a state of unrecoverable shock. His emotions had been exercised more than they had for some time, it seemed.

"No. This is a ring that I have from my father. He wore it throughout his career and gave it to me when he retired. He wore it on his pinky. I didn't want to resize it. I wear it on whatever finger it fits, either right or left ring finger."

Delores moved it to her right hand, then removed it and held it out to Chandler. "Put it on your pinky finger. I bet it fits."

Chandler hesitated. He took the ring and it slid snugly into place on his right pinky finger.

"You're right. It looks more natural on a man as well," he said.

"I wear a ring and you do not. Interesting, isn't it?"

He handed the ring to Delores.

"Here. Good Lord, this is too much. How can I be a doctor fixing hearts when I can't figure out the one in my own body? I need to go be a husband to my wife and forget about all this other crap. I trust the Lord will help you make your decision. You are a confusing and remarkable woman."

Delores did not know how to part from this man.

"Chandler, I don't know what to say or do right now."

"Neither do I."

They sat silently across from one another.

"I am going to go delete you right now, and I know I'll never forget you, Chandler Collins. My life has been changed from knowing you."

This had gone on long enough. It was time to part company. She would shake his hand. A hug would be too public and arouse suspicion.

"I am going to stand and shake your hand. You'll know what I decide very soon."

They both stood.

He reached out to shake her hand.

She took his hand.

They stared into each other's eyes and shook hands. What had just happened would take a while for each to process. Only that was clear.

"You make me want to be a better man. Thank you."

"You have helped me return to myself. Thank you."

Closure.

Chandler left the lobby and walked directly out the front doors of the Hermitage. He did not stop, and he did not look back. Delores watched him disappear from sight, then turned to the elevator and went up to her suite. She was exhausted.

Once in her room, Delores opened her laptop, logged into the matching site, and deleted Chandler swiftly. There was no need to linger or think about it. She followed through with her word. She ignored the new messages, logged out, and closed the computer.

She was not going out that evening. What she needed was time alone to calm her nerves and process the past few days. She felt very unstable. She called down for someone to draw her a hot mineral salt bath and ordered some mint tea to be delivered. In fact, Saturday would be for relaxation as well now that her business had concluded. Delores requested that arrangements be made on her behalf for a full spa package Saturday.

The staff arrived quickly to draw her bath. It was a peppermint eucalyptus mineral sea salt blend, and the scents were mixing to sooth her nerves immediately. Before getting into the tub, Delores opened her laptop once more and deleted her online matching account. It asked if she was certain she wanted to delete her profile permanently. She was certain. She clicked yes, and breathed a sigh of relief. Presenting herself as she did, which is to say dishonestly, had landed her in a precarious position through which lies could fall like dominos.

Sinking into the hot aromatic water, Delores let her mind wander. The only thing about which she was entirely certain is that she would not date Chandler. Even if he wanted to contact her, he would not be able to access her profile or send messages through the service. She was done with married men. Though she could not take back anything that had occurred in the past, her reputation would not be threatened by future indiscretions.

It would take time to process whether or not to do the work for Birdie's company. The threat existed either way, and Delores was leaning toward doing the business. If she were able to stage a fight with Birdie, an entirely different set of circumstances would emerge. At least then it would not point back to her discussion with Chandler after a perfectly amicable business lunch. To proceed with a staged argument was again going down the road of falsehood. Delores had enough of that.

She could treat Birdie as though she knew of some horrible storm that threatened her livelihood, over which neither Delores nor Birdie had any control, and the existence of which Birdie had not yet learned. In this case, it was not Delores's responsibility to disclose any information about what could be a storm or could be a simple drizzle of rain. Neither of the women had control of Chandler.

She sighed. Another thing that deeply bothered her was the conviction Chandler had about remaining married to Birdie. He was not contemplating leaving her. He was not talking badly about her. Birdie was his wife. What he did was his business. Yet, he was one more man who did not consider Delores to be marriage material.

What was it about her, she wondered, that made her undesirable as a wife? Why didn't any of her married boyfriends, or any other man for that matter, want to be married to her? She never had asked them to leave their wives. She expected that they would stay with them. Would they have considered her if they had met her first? Would they consider her if they were single? What was it like on the other side, though? Would she ever get there?

Delores sighed at the stream of questions that was running through her mind. She sipped the mint green tea and took in the scents of the eucalyptus. That is all she had to do. Breathe. Relax. Soak.

Was she going to be single forever? What would come of her when Daddy passed? When would it be her turn to be the wife? Would her husband stray? She never had considered the women on the other side of the married men she had dated. It had seemed entirely irrelevant. She wasn't trying to take them away. What would it be like, though, to be on the other side?

10 MAIZIE – NINE DAYS AGO

Eligible men hadn't exactly been springing out of the online matching service as she had hoped. She had sent two men smiles, and one had responded. After going through all the standard communication stages and a couple email messages, a match named Drew had asked her to dinner at Mastro's Ocean Club. She knew it was one of the most expensive places in the area and chuckled at its proximity to Javier's, where she first had eaten lunch with Hank. Was this a first date location featured on a checklist of some sort? What was it that led these men to believe that this was the big location that would impress the ladies?

Maizie decided to wear a slinky blue dress from the most formal of her company's product lines. She was dressed for a nice dinner in Kauai, or on another island where only a small portion of the inhabitants wore shoes at all. She pulled off casual elegance with ease, looking somehow exotic in the Newport Coast setting. Her natural hair and make-up contributed to the impression that she was visiting from a mysterious island. She embodied the perfect balance of confidence and relaxation. Her earrings and necklace were white gold with dangling pins. She liked to think of them as her dagger set. She was ready to secure her prey.

Before setting out to Mastro's, Maizie did a customary refresh of Drew's profile. She wanted to make sure to treat him according to the needs he didn't even realize he had expressed in his introduction.

Drew from Irvine, 41
Commercial Banker (Medical Field)
A long list of what is important: staying close to family & friends, my career and continuing to achieve professional success, cycling, staying in shape (easier in CA than in

Ohio for sure), being a good person who is thankful for what I have rather than what I don't have, investing in the stock market and experiencing new things. I am definitely looking for a partner to share my life with who has similar morals, values and outlook on life.

Drew had promise. He seemed like a fairly normal guy and simple to please. Being from Ohio, he would find her familiar and be won over quickly. She liked his body, which was lean and muscular in every shot. He had a full head of hair and a day job that sounded boring enough to make him listen and adapt to what she wanted in order to seem more interesting to her. That would be a bonus. It didn't appear that he had any hobbies that would annoy her immediately. He also thought he knew what he was looking for, though she was certain he actually was just looking for a woman to tell him what he wanted.

She smiled and set out in her Mini Cooper. Arriving at Mastro's she left her six-speed with the valet, entered the building, and was shown to the table she and Drew would share that evening.

Drew arrived nearly ten minutes late, and Maizie did not recognize him. Even in the dim light it was apparent that he was at least 40 pounds heavier than the pictures had indicated. He was sweating profusely. Perhaps he had chosen the restaurant for its dim lighting. It certainly was not for the view because the reservation was for just after sunset. So far the guy was not winning on any front. Perhaps he had not actually ridden his bike since he moved from Ohio.

There was one redeeming quality. He didn't have any hobbies that annoyed her, though it may be that he had no hobbies at all. He could devote all his time to her needs, at least. Maybe he was worth something.

Maizie forced a smile and stood to greet him with a gentle, distanced hug.

"So nice to meet you, Drew."

"Hi. You look absolutely stunning. I mean, your photos were outstanding, and in person you are absolutely stunning. I said that already, didn't I?"

They both took their seats. Drew fidgeted nervously. She wondered how long it had been since he had been on a date. So she asked, "Do you date much, Drew?"

He laughed nervously, and a little too loudly to be appropriate for her question. She guessed there was a great distress behind his answer.

"Yes, I do. Nothing serious though. I have been on the dating site for a while now, and there hasn't been much chemistry so far. It is tough. Well, I sure seem to have a lot of first dates. I know I do not get to ask the same question of you. That would be rude." He laughed again. It was too loud.

Yes, she was right. He was not honest with his profile. It was clear he would have only first dates unless he really stepped up his game somehow. Maybe that was the attempt with Mastro's. She decided to play with him a bit. He would either settle down or his nervousness would escalate. She didn't really care. She just wanted to see him go through some set of emotions. He was in for a ride.

"You're right. You can still ask, though. I promise I won't slap you." She winked at him.

Drew squirmed in his seat, obviously uncomfortable and not sure what to say next. Maizie stared at him with a smirk on her face and her head tilted slightly to the side.

"How long have you been on the site?" he finally asked.

Maizie sat upright and kept grinning as she responded honestly, "I have paid for this service four times in the last five years. I rarely meet anyone that I actually want to see in person. You're the first since I moved to the West Coast. It was actually a dare from my friends in Pennsylvania that has me online again."

"What kind of a dare?"

"They want to see me find someone to date for at least a month. Some of them met their husbands this way, and I just seem to not give most guys a fighting chance. I agreed."

"Why do you not give them a chance?"

"Have you ever heard of Joan of Arc? They call me Joan of Arc because I reject the common life and charge forward to conquer anyone who stands in my way."

"That is fascinating. It is hard to believe that you are single, and being called Joan of Arc is one explanation. You just are so stunning and obviously quite intelligent. I'm really flattered that you accepted my invitation. Thank you."

"You're welcome. Just so we are perfectly clear, you do not get to call me Joan."

"Of course not. There obviously is a lot more to you, but it may take a few centuries to discover it all. By then you'll be in history as Maizie of Newport Coast."

Maizie chuckled and smiled at Drew. She wondered how much he was actually worth. What did he have to offer her? She picked up the menu and selected the most expensive items from the appetizer, main, and sides.

"Well, let's toast a nice bottle of wine to that! You pick. I like red."

She knew he was now stuck. He would show his price standard and his knowledge of wine. He could play it safe and impress her with the most expensive bottle on the list, in which case he may not know wine at all. Or he could take a risk and indicate his preference and knowledge by selecting and explaining something else. If he asked, then she would know that he definitely needed to be told more specifically how he was to behave.

"Of course. I like Conundrum. It is a wonderful blended red that leaves me wanting more, and it will go with anything you order. What are you looking at?"

Maizie was impressed. Not only had he stopped squirming, Drew was showing some signs of risk taking. She remembered thinking upon first reading his profile that Drew had promise. She knew she would win him over quickly. It appeared she had been correct.

After telling him what she had selected he remained entirely calm and repeated her order to the waiter. Maizie was relieved that this man had appropriate manners that she attributed to a sign of good upbringing, confidence, and trainability. Perhaps he was loaded. She knew from the photos that his body could look incredible if she trained him to get back in shape while she investigated what his lifestyle could afford her. She was ready for an upgrade.

"What is your favorite part of living in Irvine?"

"What?"

"What is your favorite part of living in Irvine?"

"Oh, Irvine. I actually don't live in Irvine. I work there."

"Where do live, then?"

"Oh, I live just around the corner."

"In Newport Coast?"

"Yes."

"Ok. For whatever reason, you have Irvine on your profile. Newport Coast is a lot better. What is your favorite part of living in Newport Coast?"

"It is a special place to live. I'm secluded from everything and have a great view. It is also very convenient, and really quiet most of the time."

"That's why I like Laguna Beach. How did you find your home?"

She was asking as many open-ended questions as she could with a conversation that didn't flow very naturally, hoping to gather clues about Drew. It was obvious that he was taken by her, and that he still was distracted by his attraction to her. As the evening progressed, Maizie came to believe that she was in the company of a very successful man.

He initially seemed to be undesirable because he no longer had the body that he had when the pictures on his profile were taken. What she found attractive was his confidence and knowing that he had been attractive, and that at one point he could have had any woman he wanted. He was not aware of his part in the frequent one-date-only encounters. He still thought of himself as someone entirely different than the image he currently showed the world.

After the meal, they shared their third bottle of Conundrum, a wine that turned out to be incredibly true to his description, leaving her wanting more. She wanted more of Drew as well. At midnight, it clearly was time to leave Mastro's. They were among the last half dozen customers remaining.

Drew walked Maizie to the valet. She was curious what he drove. Her Mini Cooper was delivered, and Drew motioned to the valet to allow him to walk her to the car. At the door, he asked if she would see him for dinner the following Saturday at Tabu in South Laguna Beach. She said she had to check her calendar, and thanked him for the dinner.

She moved in for a distant hug like the one they'd exchanged when he first had arrived. As she leaned back from the hug, though, she let her cheek graze his and turned her head slightly so he would feel the shape of her lips on his cheek. It was subtle. He would want more, and he wouldn't know exactly what it was that had him wanting it so badly. He just stood there.

She got in her car and drove swiftly through the parking lot around to the other side of the building. She pulled into a row of the parking lot beside a large SUV so that she would be able to spy on him getting into his own car. When Drew turned the opposite way in a Bentley, Maizie was satisfied with his financial status.

He was totally taken with her, and she would move forward very carefully with him. He had to think he was fighting to get her. She was going to make him work like a dog. He would like it. It was just the beginning of the fighting he would have to do to keep her, though at any point he would not even know what was going on with the spell she had cast. He would be trained. It would start with him following up on the dinner invitation.

11 MAIZIE – LAST SATURDAY

Maizie was in good spirits when she woke up on Saturday. She also was without plans for the evening. This would have to be changed. She wanted a nice dinner. She took her laptop and walked down the hill to the corner coffee shop. She could gaze at the ocean and watch the customers passing through the busy corner location while she looked at the prospects for the evening, though most of the ones who had contacted her she had deemed ineligible.

Maizie had been in Laguna Beach for a few weeks, and it had become evident quickly that her salary and desired lifestyle were greatly mismatched. While perks like free clothing in the latest styles helped, it would be very difficult to reach any standard of living that was of interest without a boost. It was becoming increasingly annoying to see scores of exotic cars passing each day and not to have her own.

Plenty of successful men were around who would be willing to give her whatever she wanted if they could sleep with her. She just had to get them sold on the package before they realized for themselves that they were in over their heads. It would be clear which one to lock into a "relationship" when the assets were analyzed and she determined which had the greatest offering.

There was a level she had identified as the minimal threshold, and her experience with Jared had set that higher and stricter than it had been before. While there were no exceptions, there was a chance that she would uncover a decent guy with a little more investigation. There was always the possibility that a new match was interesting.

Her inbox contained a few communication requests to sift through first.

Herb from Huntington Beach, 42
Recycling Management
I split time between Northern Ca. and Orange County, I have sucessfully managed relationships that involved distance. I would always go out of my way to spend time with someone I cared about and hope they would do the same for me even if it took effort :-).

Really? That one was a simple decision. No. She needed to have full access to his life, and splitting was not something that would work. He had to be there for her when she wanted. It sounded like Herb wanted the woman to take the effort to go visit him. Why? And recycling management sounded very.... blue collar. Delete.

Randy from Newport Beach, 44
Medical
I think getting to know someone in person is more exciting and fun than just reading about it.

Well, that is interesting. Maizie agreed entirely, and she also needed more information before spending any time in person with Randy as with anyone. If nothing else, he would likely be willing to take her out the same night. She quickly responded to his questions and sent her own. She didn't think he would care what she wrote back. She was willing to bet that his was a game of numbers in which he wanted one girl out of 20-30 to write back at all. He had to start fighting to get her out tonight. He would be thrilled, in fact, to have the opportunity.

Sterling from Costa Mesa, 40
Finance
I have many interests especially travel and history. Now that i have gotten better at golf I enjoy playing a few times a month as well as hiking and mountain biking. I enjoy hiking because it is a great workout and a good time for conversation as well. Other hobbies I enjoy are football, Basketball, Soccer and softball.

Just reading those three lines she pegged Sterling as a bore, and an unsuccessful one with poor writing skills at that. Delete.

Joe from Corona del Mar, 40
Executive VP
The paticulars: I pride myself on being intelligent, and educated but I feel that a sense of humor, charm, compassion and enjoying life as much as possible are far more endearing qualities. I snowboard, wakeboard, surf, golf, fish and love to travel. I'm in the office most of the day, and I like to spend my nights/weekends outside. I do enjoy cooking in

my free time (bowls of cereal do not qualify). Yes a guy that can cook; amazing huh? I currently work as an Executive for a large IT Company and have the opportunity to travel quite a bit both for work and pleasure. I currently live in Corona del Mar and absolutely love it here!

Joe seemed okay if not a little too enthusiastic. As an executive he probably brought home a large enough salary to suit her expanding desires. His strong suit was that he stated he worked in an office and wanted to have something different outside the office. He also sounded like he was newer in town, which may make him more malleable to her. Maizie answered his questions and sent her own. He may be outside, as his profile stated he liked to be when not working.

Mario from Laguna Hills, 40
Automotive Maintenance Specialist for Exotic Cars
I am passionate about travel. Going to different places, experiencing cultures... I really gather a sense of appreciation for diversity and individuality. Tasting local cuisine and listening to local music are some of my favorite things to do when I'm on an adventure. Rarely do I participate in the touristy activities, but sometimes they are a treat. Just put me in a place where I can absorb the sights, sounds, and smells (with caution) and I would feel right at home. James 1:2-3, "... when troubles come your way, consider it an opportunity for great joy. For you know that when your faith is tested, your endurance has a chance to grow."

A bible-toting mechanic? Delete! There was no way that she wanted any part in that.

She was done looking.

As expected Randy had sent back his answers to her questions within ten minutes. She let him sit for a while and gazed out at the ocean. As much as she loved to look at the ocean, it was only the one time in Fiji that she actually had gone in it. Something about it made her nervous. She did not like feeling nervous. It was just so much more powerful than her. Fear of being less powerful was not a feeling she appreciated in herself. From her seat it did not pose any threat to her, and she was able to absorb its power. That was a feeling that was welcome any time.

Twenty minutes after sending his answers, Randy sent a request to skip the rest of the standard communication steps and go right to the mail exchange. Maizie snickered at how accurately she had judged Randy from that simple message. She let him wait longer, and went to the counter for a refill of her signature blend coffee.

With a fresh cup of coffee at her side, Maizie accepted Randy's request to move directly to the mail exchange. She knew that the silly warning would appear from the site, indicating that she should be aware of matches who said or did anything from a list the site identified with abusers of the service, and that it ultimately was her responsibility to ensure she was safe with her date. To her, it was the cleverest release of liability she ever had seen. The service was making full disclosure of things to watch out for, like a match claiming it was fate or moving too fast. The users did what people always did by ignoring rather than reading the contents. Idiots!

Randy's message was simple.

'Hi, Maizie. Thanks for your response. What made you respond to an older guy?'

'Hi Randy. It's easier to sift through the nonsense in person! And fun, too ;)'

She had stepped outside her normal bounds with the winking smiley face. It seemed like the best way to get to the casual communication that she guessed Randy was seeking.

'lol'

'I'm about to walk out the door. Talk to you later.'

'how about later?'

'pretty busy today'

'i want to meet you. u look so interesting and beautiful'

'What did you have in mind? Send me a message and I'll get back to you. Running out the door now. Bye.'

Maizie was happy to have her backup in place. He certainly would be trying to figure out a way to get her to dinner, and he knew it had to be compelling. If he did nothing, it would surprise her. He seemed like a local, though wasn't her type. Still, she wanted to get out and get more experience with Southern California men. It was a different breed here. She wanted to understand it and know the rules they were expecting.

At 6 pm Maizie was getting ready for her date with Joe. He had written back at lunch from work, which he said was not normal for a Saturday. He was far more stable than Randy, who could be a backup during the week. Randy wanted to get laid. He would jump at the chance to see her any time.

Joe was taking her to Fleming's in Newport Beach. It was not entirely original, though she knew it was a nice setting with a superb menu for prime steak, seafood, and wine. They would sit close to one another and have the time truly to themselves. She wore the same blue dress from the previous night's outing to Mastro's. It felt a little like a uniform, so she had made sure to wear her sexiest underwear. She wanted to remember her underwear to bring out a larger smile and more mischief in her conversation with Joe.

When she arrived Joe was waiting for her at the bar in khakis and a white dress shirt. He didn't have a belt. His blonde hair was combed with too much styling product, and he looked like he was trying his hardest to appear a couple steps above his pedigree. She wondered what that was.

The hostess fetched him, and led the two of them to a nice quiet table in the far rear corner. Her brisk efficiency prevented the standard awkward hug and greeting, so they said hello to one another on the way to the table. Once they slid into the plush booth, they both were smiling. They were able to laugh about the rush. It already was so much more natural than the night before with Drew.

As the evening wore on, the conversation flowed easily. They continued to smile at one another, and Maizie let herself laugh heartily. Joe was a fun time guy, and it was easy to be around him. He was a great subject from which to learn about men in Southern California.

Maizie felt empowered with Joe. He was eager to follow her lead in the conversation, and she knew he would be a great catch for someone. The difficulty came in assessing his path compared to her date the previous night.

Drew was absolutely solid in his career and definitely had begun a path to great success. Fine things were familiar to him, and he downplayed his success. Joe was less predictable. He was new in his position, and as nice as he was he was very shallow. There was not much to him. Even if he became consumed with her, she was not certain he would have the depth to remain committed to her needs if any part of his career was ever uncomfortable.

Joe seemed like he would be susceptible to having a midlife crisis before he climbed higher. She could picture him coming home one day to explain that he had quit his job, plunging into a depression out of which he would expect her to raise him. He would not provide sufficiently.

Perhaps the simplest terms to describe his character were: weak, spineless, impressionable, temporary. How long would she need him? That would depend what he actually had to offer. Tonight would be it. He was good simply for dinner and a flirtatious hug like she had given Drew.

Joe drove a BMW 335 coupe. Not a Bentley. He was an odd mix of new money and outdated standards, and he may never grow into the role of a man of wealth or importance. His connections definitely came from his poor days.

12 DELORES – LAST SUNDAY

After a relaxing day at the spa on Saturday, Delores was done with Nashville. Sunday morning, the car delivered her to the private jet at the airport. As she boarded, she was quite aware of a whirlpool of negative feelings that had subsided just to allow a larger whirlpool of fear to take precedence.

Delores was pleased to have two, and possibly three, lucrative ventures lined up for her corporation. She had decided that proceeding with Birdie was her chosen course of action.

It was not for the money. Delores had plenty of money, and her corporation had made profit every year since its inception.

It was not for Birdie. Delores was not attached to Birdie. She did not want to be malicious toward the woman, and she did not pity her.

It was not for Chandler. His character would be revealed soon enough, and fortunately nothing would be traceable back to Delores at this point.

She respected what Birdie wanted to do. Delores wanted to connect the funds with groups that would use the money for the greater good of society. Her obsession with the conservation of each cent overtook any fear of Birdie finding out about Chandler's secret life. She had already lined up the recipients.

One other contract with Dolly had been returned to the hotel, signed, on Saturday. Bunny had yet to return the contract. Chloe would have to follow up with her on Monday.

What was bothering Delores now was the state of her father's mental health, and his health overall. The nurse had mentioned he was less lucid the past couple days. Perhaps he would turn around.

Delores had hoped they could have a nice visit when she returned to the standard 2 pm meeting time Sunday. Then he did not even register that she had entered the room. He was in his own world, and she was not part of it at all. She just wanted so badly to believe he could turn around.

Delores knew better.

No matter what she knew she would never have her daddy back.

The worry was carried along through the evening. The whirlpool was gaining strength. She knew she would be all alone in the world very soon. She was terrified. It was hard to breathe.

Staring out over the Pacific Ocean from the house in Newport Coast, she decided to create a new profile with her real name on the dating site. She was not ready to let go of the hope of a husband for herself, and she certainly was not meeting men organically. She chose to believe in success and believe that she could have another chapter of pure happiness in her life with a man other than her daddy.

She threw a ball a few times for Ferdi and Polly, and then asked for her laptop when Nelda came out to feed the dogs.

Determined, Delores created a new profile for herself. The questions seemed endless, and there were so many similarities among the questions. Instead of getting distracted by the process, Delores answered question after question with no delay. The first thing that came to her mind was what went in the rating box. She was able to complete the entire registration within thirty minutes. She used the same photos. She decided she would pay for a year with a $500 prepaid credit card. While it was more honest than using a fake name with Wendy's billing, she was still able to protect herself from the danger of cyber stalkers. Protecting her corporation and identity was still important. She would continue to do that until she knew she could trust someone to enter her life.

The whirlpool was churning again. It seemed to be gaining speed. She took a deep breath, and after a few moments retreated to bed early. A ride in the morning would feel great after six days off the bike.

13 DELORES – LAST MONDAY

After a wonderful ride up and down the coast on Monday, Delores was sitting on the patio enjoying breakfast and coffee while stealing curious glances at her laptop ever few minutes. Finally, when she had finished her breakfast and could stand it no more, she opened the laptop and logged on to the dating site to see if she had any matches on her new profile. The whirlpool had not disappeared yet, though at least it had subsided for a few hours.

She saw that she had eighteen matches, and one who wanted to communicate. He had sent her an icebreaker with a note saying her profile had brought a smile to his face. She thought that was sweet and opened his profile to learn more about him.

Lawrence from Laguna Beach, 44
Managing Director
I was in a 23 year relationship that started when I was in college, and now I am looking for a successful independent woman to share in the next phase of my life as the chapter unfolds. Honesty, integrity, humility, and genuine character are four of the most important mutual values to me. My ideal partner would have been in a committed long term relationship and will understand that I am a career man and an excellent father who is actively involved in my kids' daily lives. At the same time I enjoy sharing dinner and a bottle of wine with a lovely lady on a romantic evening.

He sounded so normal and communicated so clearly. He had balance in multiple aspects of his life and was able to express himself in a way that was straightforward to her. From his profile he looked like he understood the value of hard work, and placed tremendous energy in his family. His profile indicated he might want to have more children. That was good enough for Delores. If it were a definite no, that would have been problematic.

There was a strong connection to his career in finance, and she appreciated that. Plus he was located nearby along the coast. She wanted to continue living by the coast, and this made it convenient. She would not consider another match outside her immediate surroundings. Her life was here. She needed to be near her father.

There was a photo of Lawrence with two children, a boy and a girl perhaps two years younger than the boy. Even though the photo was set in the woods during a 10k run, they were quite clean, obviously well groomed on a regular basis. That said a lot to her about his personal standards. The children appeared happy and to be kind, loving, and polite. Lawrence had a warm smile on his face that emanated love for the two children. He had a hand on the shoulder of each child. Delores examined his hands. They looked large and gentle, and the way they rested so softly on the children's shoulders made them look like a comfortable and peaceful family. He appeared to be a gentle, humble man.

Delores clicked on the button to return the smile to Lawrence. She was going to move slowly. A returned smile would allow Lawrence to make the next move.

The whirlpool of fear and anxiety was running again.

At 10:00 in the morning a notification appeared on her computer to indicate she had received a message. Delores opened the service site and read a series of five questions from Lawrence. She answered without much thought, and sent him back a set of five questions of her own. They both had asked about preferred schedule, level of affection, and philosophy on travel. It seemed superficial, yet she trusted the process.

She was prompted to send lists of the characteristics she needed and those she refused in a partner.

Just after lunch another notification appeared to indicate she had a message on the service site. Lawrence had sent his two lists. Delores scanned them and realized they were the same as hers.

As she was about to close the service site when she received another message. She went to her inbox and saw one from another man. She gave his profile a glance.

Hank from Laguna Beach, 42
Biotech M&A
I am passionate about my career, traveling and being genuine to others. I absolutely love new adventures and am looking for someone with whom to share those. I'm looking for a

partner who wants to share her life, travel, and explore new things. I want to find someone who is not afraid to be herself. She has passions, desires and drive, and also a witty/silly side to her. Above all, I want to be with someone who is kind and sincere. Coming from the East Coast two years ago I want to find a genuine lady who is interested in direct and honest communication. I am trusting that there is a proverbial needle in the haystack who will be delivered as a match so we can take a deep breath and start out on our journey together.

The caliber of matches certainly had increased since she had put in an honest name. Delores was charmed by the vibrant qualities of Hank. It seemed like Laguna Beach was her hot spot, which was a relief. Venturing inland in Orange County was not an idea that sat well with her unless it was part of a bike ride. It had to be temporary and purpose-driven. Laguna Beach provided a suitable lifestyle, and she was confident these two men had high enough standards at least to engage in conversation.

Before she could respond to Hank's questions, Delores was interrupted by an incoming message from Lawrence. He wanted to skip the rest of the standard steps set up by the site and proceed directly to the mail exchange. Delores figured she may as well proceed, and she clicked on the 'Accept Invitation' button. A pop-up appeared that advised her of safety, reiterating the fact that the standard steps had been set up for a reason. She read no further than that headline and dismissed the popup. She had a conference call starting in a couple minutes and wanted to read the message so she could return her full focus to work for the next hour.

'Hi, Delores. Your profile makes me smile. You look very nice.'

That was simple. Delores did not type anything.

Her desk line was ringing. She closed the browser and got to work on the call.

Immediately after the call, Delores decided to answer Hank's questions first, then send her own, and finally respond to Lawrence's simple message. To her surprise there was already another note from Lawrence.

'Rare to meet someone from the coast, is it not?'

Delores decided to mirror his style and keep her reply simple.

'Hi Lawrence. Thank you for your kind words. Yes, it is rare.'

Send.

She clicked over to Hank and answered his questions. They were the same she had been asked by Lawrence, so it was easy for her to send the same set of answers again, though this time to Hank. She sent him the same questions.

She noticed how consumed she had become by the service now that she had decided to give it an honest chance. She had to get to her father's. She decided she would not check the service again until tomorrow, even if messages popped up for her.

14 DELORES – LAST TUESDAY

When Delores opened the service site on Tuesday after breakfast, she had received a message from Lawrence.

'How was your day?'

She was struck by the simplicity of his message. She did not know the last time she had answered such a basic question. It felt good to be asked.

'Good morning. My day was nice. How was your day?'

Delores closed the computer with the intent to open it again after lunch. Instead she got sidetracked with calls and did not have time before going to visit her father. At seven o'clock that evening there was a message from Lawrence.

'Great :) It was better because you sent me a message. Would you be interested in meeting me for coffee this weekend? I can meet you at the Crystal Cove shopping center. We live so close, it seems getting to know each other in person would be easier than a couple sentences a day. Speaking of days, I hope yours is going well.'

Well, that was direct. She had nothing to lose. Coffee was light and public, and it was easy to walk away if it he was not interesting.

'Yes, that would be nice. I am available on Saturday.'

She was curious what Lawrence was like.

Less then an hour passed before she received his response.

'Name the time and place and I will be there.'

On Saturday she would want to get a ride in and not deviate from her regular morning routine, except for limiting herself to only half a cup of coffee at home. She was already feeling like he would be a good friend. Even if they did not hit it off he was very compassionate. It was somehow romantic how he offered to meet when it was convenient to her.

'I'll see you at Starbucks at Crystal Cove at 9 am Saturday.' It never hurt to be specific. 'Goodnight,' she added, and sent the message.

15 DELORES – LAST WEDNESDAY

When Delores opened the service site on Tuesday after breakfast, she had received a message from Lawrence. She was beginning to enjoy the morning message. It was something she felt comfortable adding to her morning routine. Reading the message gave her reason to ride harder and longer, and to smile the whole time in anticipation of who this man was.

'That is perfect. I look forward to seeing you there. You can text or call me at 949-555-2345 from now on if that is easier. I hope you had a wonderful night of sleep. Have a great day.'

Delores did not write anything back, and went about her day. She was not accustomed to sending text messages and viewed them more as a means for specific data-driven communication, like when, where, what. She did not approve of the way texting had replaced the phone, and at the same time she was willing to do something a little different in that regard since she already was embracing online dating. She did not know how this worked. Perhaps the whole thing was meant to be electronic until they actually met or knew each other.

For the second day in a row, Delores was consumed by her work and did not check her matching service account during the day. She knew that would get very dangerous in terms of reducing her productivity.

After dinner she opened her computer to the service site and found a message from Hank. He had answered her questions, and actually seemed like a very kind and stable man. She sent him her two lists. As she was closing his profile she received a message from Lawrence.

'How was your day?'

Delores smiled. The regular electronic companionship was winning her favor. Instead of replying on the service, she picked up her cell phone and texted.

'Hi Lawrence. My day was great. How was yours? -Delores'

She turned off her phone. It was near her bedtime, so she prepared herself as usual and got into bed. Even though she wouldn't get a response from Lawrence right away, through the most instant method of communication, she was more excited about seeing a message from him in the morning. He seemed so compassionate, and she could envision being great friends with him even if there was no chemistry romantically.

She had forgotten about Hank entirely.

16 MAIZIE – LAST WEDNESDAY

Maizie wrapped up a personal training session with her new trainer at a private gym and began the short walk back to her hillside apartment. She had found the best trainer yet, and that was tough given how picky she always had been with her devoted trainers. They all liked to train her because she was a different specimen entirely, remaining stoic under routines that others would not dream to attempt.

Living in Laguna Beach, she had a lot of competition from women who made it their primary purpose to be attractive and fit. Some of them were waifs that she saw drifting through town. Others were at the gym two times each day to ensure they were in better shape than anyone else in their social circle and that they remained attractive to their husbands.

At the same time the men were fighting against each other to be the alpha male or the most attractive, fit man in town. Money was not a large enough differentiator. They wanted to have the most money and the best body so they could have any woman they wanted. With all the money that was floating around the ten-mile strip of the coast, cost of training was not the issue. Maizie set her sights on the most exclusive private gym, and that is where she had been going since the week she moved into her new apartment.

Maizie had negotiated with the owner of the private gym, who was also her trainer, to give her three sessions at no cost and then set a rate that was fair for both. Rick was used to seeing and touching gorgeous women, so it was a different set of bargaining that she had to employ. She told him she would not pay more than half what the other women paid, and promised that she would pre-pay for three months of sessions if he would work her hard enough that their partnership would be worthwhile. After three weeks, they both were smitten with the 25% rate he was charging and the camaraderie that had formed. Maizie would talk about the dates she was going on, and she was listening constantly for a clue to a single and wealthy client whom she could meet through Rick. So far it was only married men, and that would do her no good.

Showering and changing into fresh loungewear, Maizie considered the reconnaissance mission she was on to find her next "boyfriend". It was painstaking, and she was learning so much about the odd dating culture in Orange County. There was so much to learn.

Her matches through the online service were mediocre at best. It seemed that they only would serve as a launching point, allowing her to elevate her social status to the millionaire level quickly and then find the next step to multi-millionaire matches through that new circle. Her sphere of influence would have to increase slowly, drawing on all of her patience.

Given the size of the county and its variations, as well as the swift increase in the number of matches she was getting, Maizie had devised a method for reducing the number of profiles she looked at on the matching service site. She did not want to waste any time in this search.

She pulled out the map of Orange County that she had purchased at the corner gas station on Sunday. The smallest radius on the matching site was 30 miles, so that was the reach of the matches. She was glad that she was directly on the coast and only had to look at half of the circle. She had marked zones in various colors so she could sort the matches into the appropriate categories in seconds rather than minutes.

After her experience at the extended suites she had no intention of affiliating with a man who lived in an area that was even the slightest bit beneath her preferred standards. She would not be spending any time in such areas. The thought of spending an evening or a weekend there was absolutely unacceptable.

Instead of driving through the county to evaluate, she had done research as though she would be buying a home. Really she was looking to own a man rather than a home.

A large section of the map she had marked red based on the demographics and income of residents in those areas. Any match from those cities was closed instantly. There was no need to think. It was a simple action based on what she knew, even if the photo was appealing. Delete. There had been a snag in this since she could only delete matches with whom she was communicating.

It amused her that the workaround included teasing these men, who never would have a chance with her. She would initiate communication with them, either through sending a message asking to bypass the standard steps of the service or by sending a list of five questions. Immediately after sending she would have the ability to delete the match. That is exactly what she did. She was getting it down to under 20 seconds. This was a huge improvement.

Also on the map was a medium sized collection of pink zones that she would place in her archive. While they were not dismissed immediately, they were out of sight. These were the areas that were definitely in the smallest economic sphere increase and would be suitable for a couple of dates in case she was out of others. These matches mostly bored or angered her with their utter uselessness other than to feed her.

Finally there was a green zone. Maizie also was amused that the color green could be used here to indicate both 'go' and 'money'. The green zone included the 10 mile strip from Newport Beach to Dana Point, extending inland one half mile. There were a handful of small sections that extended further inland at Corona del Mar, Newport Coast, and the guard gated communities along the coast highway in Laguna Beach. She knew of a few cities inland that met her standards, and these were marked green zones as well.

The system was not perfect because the zip codes extended slightly into less desirable areas. For the most part, though, it seemed like the best way to keep it efficient and effective.

After sorting through the 15 matches and communicating with those who made the map cut, she also responded to Drew. She would go to dinner with him on Saturday. He had the most to offer at this point. Besides, if a better one came along she would be able to make him work to get a date set up without playing any games. This was easy. More quality matches always arrived when she was less available.

17 DELORES – LAST THURSDAY

Delores was excited to see if Lawrence had replied to her message. Before her ride, she had not looked for a reply. When she returned, there were two text messages from Lawrence. Last night he had written back.

'Good :) goodnight.'

The second had been sent at 6:18 am. Delores was happy to see he was active in the early morning.

'Good morning :) I'm looking forward to meeting you. What are you up to today?'

'I just finished a 35 mile bike ride. Today is a typical business day. What are your plans for the day?'

'Oh, that is a long bike ride. I'm impressed. You must be in great shape. Do you ride every morning?'

'This was a short ride. I like to get out on my bike 5 days per week when I'm in town.'

'You have a lot in common with my older boy. He just got a new road bike so he can do jr ironman. Can't get him off of it ;) Poor guy is confined to a pretty small area until he finds a club'

'How old is he? I saw photos of you with your kids on a run. Do you run a lot?'

':) Yes. I train half the year for 2 races. One is a marathon I do alone. Big Sur. Other is with kids. Boys 13, 11. Girl 8. They are all swimmers. Oldest boy is a real athlete.'

'It's clear you have a strong connection with them. I admire that.'

'Thank you :) How long have u lived in NC?'

The smiley faces and abbreviation threw Delores off balance slightly. She would have to learn to speak text, and that was fine. Abbreviations were not foreign to her.

'2 yrs. Lived in Beverly Hills before, and my main office is there. I mostly stay here by the coast.'

'It is a special place. I have been in NB/CDM for last 20 yrs, and Laguna as of 2 yrs ago.'

'Yes, the coast is special and very peaceful. I just feel good here'

Delores looked at her watch and realized she had been texting for nearly 45 minutes! No wonder she was hungry. Instead of waiting for his response, she got in the shower and started to move on with her rather busy workday.

During breakfast, Delores noticed that the whirlpool of emotions she was experiencing from her trip to Nashville had disappeared. When had it gone? She did not even recall. Was it from being back at her father's side each afternoon? After being away from him the previous week, her worrying was lessened just by seeing him daily. It did not matter whether he was coherent or oblivious to her presence.

She was comforted knowing everyone was doing his or her best to care for him. Following through with her request for an update each day while she was away had made Delores certain that the staff did care and actually was looking after his needs. It would have been easy for them to send a one-line note that said 'Fine' or 'No change', just copying and pasting from the previous message. Instead they told her the truth in a manner that did not alarm her or cause worry. They were professionals, and she respected that.

Was it Lawrence? She really enjoyed the attention and its regularity. It was exciting to be meeting a local man. She hadn't dated anyone in Orange County for quite some time.

Was it work? With the three new contracts, it was a much more demanding daily schedule. Chloe was a tremendous help, though Delores was not used to the grind and to courting the new organizations to learn what interests they really represented. It wasn't simple to get the financials from some of them, and the courtship was delicate.

Whatever it was, Delores was glad that the whirlpool had gone just as quickly as it had arrived. It was a discomfort she had not experienced many times in her life. She hoped it would be kept at bay.

After lunch, Delores went to retrieve her cell phone to see if any new text messages had arrived from Lawrence. She imagined they had. It was an odd transition for her to be looking at a device for a source of excitement, and that is exactly what she realized she was doing.

And there it was.

'Delores, I am going to Pelican Hill this afternoon for a business meeting. Would you like to meet for a drink afterward in lieu of coffee?'

She thought about it. Pelican Hill is where she had met Chandler, only this time Lawrence had chosen. She was impressed by his invitation and found it amusing she had chosen it originally to allow for the impression of a business meeting, which Lawrence was conducting there that day. They had similar taste. She smiled.

'Yes, I am available after 7 pm.'

Instantly, a response appeared.

'Wonderful. I can't wait to meet you. Have a great afternoon :)'

She smiled at his smiley face punctuation, and headed out to see her father. She wondered if her excitement would register with him. It seemed he was slipping further away from her each day, and she was glad that there was something to pull her back from the edge of the cliff of loss at which she certainly would find herself in the next few years.

Delores prepared to meet Lawrence that evening. It was a lot of Lawrence in a single day. She had not taken much time to consider how she felt about his kids: three kids between eight and thirteen. She wondered what had happened with his marriage. Whatever it was, it seemed it must have been very serious for them to part ways with three school-aged children at home. Delores had been told many times that a couple really has to want a divorce in order to go through with it. One of her friends had likened it to being beat up by your best friend nearly every single day for two years. That was a friend who had no children, and whose husband had seemed perfectly charming.

She decided to just be herself and let Lawrence be himself. She felt pretty certain that as long as he didn't drink too much, he would be a great catch. Delores wore a raw silk skirt in a light honey color and a black tank with black raw silk heels. This outfit was sexy, and it also gave her a professional edge. To soften the professional look, she let her silky, honey blond hair fall over her shoulders and touched up her makeup to accentuate smoky eyes and shapely lips. She went back into her closet and selected a raspberry and black silk scarf and a raspberry clutch. The addition of color with the scarf was an uplifting finishing touch. She chose diamond earrings and a diamond tennis bracelet, both set in gold, and removed her father's ring.

For the second time in two weeks, she smiled at her reflection in the mirror on the way to her car, and in the rear view mirror on her way to Pelican Hill. She felt desirable and desired. Life was very good.

A text message buzzed through on her phone. A slight panic flashed through her. Was Lawrence canceling? She reached for her phone to read the message. It was from Lawrence.

'I'm done with my meeting. See you at 7.'

'I'm on my way.'

Again, Delores was greeted by Pedro, who opened the door of her Tesla and extended his hand to assist her as she stepped out. The valet was happy to see her again, and smiled genuinely.

Delores paused to take a deep breath before entering the clubhouse. She closed her eyes and took five more deep breaths to calm herself and allow that calm to flow through her body. She remembered how gorgeous she looked at that moment, opened her eyes, and walked to the grand front entrance. The massive doors were opened for her, and she walked in with her head held high in confidence.

In the lobby, she spotted Lawrence. She thought it was kind that he had waited in the lobby instead of the bar. He was wearing a silver suit, shinier than her taste would have preferred. A black dress shirt, unbuttoned at the top, was clean and crisp. His eyes were shining with life, and his smile made him very welcoming. He saw her, and his smile grew to stretch from ear to ear.

Lawrence was quite handsome. His black hair was neatly cut and combed. His skin was a healthy tan, and his face was square, strong, and cleanly shaven. He was slightly slimmer than he had appeared in the pictures, and just as warm looking. His eyebrows had an arc shape that brought cheer to his face. His broad shoulders made him seem cuddly like a big stuffed bear. There was a subtle yet distinct vulnerability to him.

"Hello," he said.

His voice was slightly higher than she had anticipated. It made him seem friendlier yet.

"Hi."

He held out his hand and she took it lightly in hers, not shaking. He didn't shake either. It seemed natural given their attire, though she had expected a hug. He was so genuine. She was immediately at ease in his presence.

"I thought we could sit in the lounge and enjoy a drink. It is really quiet in there, so we can actually hear each other speak."

She followed his lead to the lounge and to a table in the corner that overlooked the courtyard and the setting sun over the Pacific Ocean. This was a nice touch.

"And as a bonus we get to watch the sunset. That is, you can watch it. I mostly will be enjoying my view of you."

"I love watching the sunset at my house. Do you watch it much?"

"Not as much as I'd like to, no. I appreciate it. I live right by the beach and have a view. It is easy to go down and watch from the sand when I make it home on time. That is my favorite."

"I rarely go to the beach. Do you spend much time there?"

"Believe me, it is the best thing to do to occupy the kids. I want them to appreciate what they have. Not everyone gets this kind of lifestyle, and it is very important to me that they look around and acknowledge their blessings. At the beach I mostly keep an eye on them. With three I am totally outnumbered. They are really good kids, though."

"I imagine the sunset is a luxury, then. How often do you have custody of your kids?"

"Usually I have them Wednesday and every other weekend. It does vary a little. In the summer I keep them overnight Wednesday, and during the school year they need to be at their mother's to get up and ready for school on time." He paused thoughtfully. "Do you have or want kids?"

Delores thought a moment.

"I want the option to have kids. It isn't something I had considered seriously until recently. I don't want to realize in a few years that I missed my chance to be a mother."

Lawrence nodded.

"I would have a hard time with someone who didn't like kids or definitely did not want kids. I love kids. I guess that's because I am a family guy 100%. I believe in marriage. I believe in strong relationships and open communication. I am not as interested in superficial things, or things that don't last like looks, sex, and material possessions. Any of those things come and go. To me it is the values that matter. That is what lasts. I want a partner to share my life with and who understands we will have some variation in how we perceive each other. I believe in commitment, and in working through things together."

He spoke with conviction and was so grounded in his description of family and values. Delores was relieved that was out of the way and that she did not have to ask many questions to get the answers. She did hope that he was sexual enough, though, having mentioned that it was not a primary interest in a relationship.

"I agree. A mentor told me to have a relationship in college, regardless what happened. She said that it was important to have that because it would be a significant learning experience. I decided to start a business instead, and my boyfriends were short-lived. I have had several longer relationships, and now I am ready to establish myself in a committed relationship that could lead to marriage. When I make a commitment, I take it very seriously."

Lawrence chuckled.

"I had that college relationship. When two people are 18 and 20 their hormones are raging, they are away from home for the first time, and it can seem like a match made in heaven. Sometimes values change as we discover who we are in the world. People can drift apart until there is nothing left even though that image of what once was remains strong. At some point I had to break away and realize I was chasing a dream that no longer was possible because we were two different people with values that had long ago diverged."

"That must have been difficult."

"Yes, it was. It has been a couple years since the marriage was over, though, and it is so much better now. When I am with the kids, I am actually capable of being present to them. It certainly was not possible before. They are doing so much better now, at least when they are with me. I hope it is the same with their mother. I don't really know what goes on over there, though."

She decided to change the subject from his children to himself as a child. "Tell me about your parents. What was it like growing up with them?"

"My parents have been married for 52 years. I'm an only child. They live in Vail, Colorado, now, but I grew up on the East Coast. Actually we were all up and down the East Coast. They worked a lot and we were pretty much a normal working class family. I had to work for everything that I have. I wasn't a latchkey kid only because I was out making money and playing sports. La Crosse turned out to be my sport. Actually, I got scholarships to several schools for La Crosse. Everyone thought I was crazy to come to California. I had already decided at age 15 that I would come here as soon as I was 18, and I followed through."

He glanced at the sunset for a moment and returned his eyes to Delores.

"I was drawn to the ocean and the lifestyles of the rich and famous. I had some inclination to marry a wealthy older lady and be her pool boy so I would never have to work. That didn't quite work out. I love economics and finance. I love finding patterns in things and making money grow. There were times I despised my parents because they never gave me what the other kids had. Now I am grateful because I know how to take care of business. I would say I have done quite well. Whatever comes next I can handle with grace and dignity."

"That is incredible. I respect that you have that work ethic. It's rare in Southern California especially," she said.

"Thank you. Now it is your turn. What was your family like?"

"I grew up mostly with my father. He traveled frequently and sometimes took me along. I loved going to Europe and even just to Riverside. When I was growing up Riverside was wide open without the smog, and I could ride a horse as though I was a cowgirl."

Delores smiled at the memory.

"I grew up amidst the beauty of the same things you are teaching your kids to appreciate. My dad taught me that. It's great that you are teaching your kids the same. He also taught me about business and made sure I created my own. He said our legacies were to be separate since our dreams were different. He lives nearby, and I see him regularly. I didn't have a lot of time with my mother, so I treasure what I have with him, especially now that he is older. I spent so many years working, traveling, and just living my own life. I like having him in it."

"He obviously means a lot to you."

"Yes."

"I admire that you are a trailblazer. You know how to dream. A lot of women only know how to spend and have no appreciation for what it takes to make it. I am not an ATM. I tell my kids that all the time. I am really glad to see proof that it works!"

Delores smiled.

The conversation flowed easily, and it seemed like they had more in common with each passing subject.

"Have you been using the service for very long?" he asked.

"This is my second time using it. Last time I met one man, and it just didn't work out. How long have you been using the service?"

"Oh, off and on for a while. I have met some incredible women. There just hasn't been anyone that was really compatible for the long term. You have to be careful. There are people out there with ulterior motives."

"Yes, I think you are right about that," Delores agreed, thinking of her recent experience with Chandler.

"I really am glad that you could come out tonight. It looks like I have the kids this weekend. At least I have two of them for sure, so I won't be available. Delores, I enjoy your company and getting to know you. Can I keep in touch this weekend even though we will have to wait until next week to get together again?"

"Of course. I would like that. It is nice to get your smiley faces. I am glad to have a face to the text now."

"Right! Now you can picture me smiling when you get a message," he teased.

She laughed. "I really do have to get going. I didn't realize it is nearly 10 pm."

"I know! I am usually a good judge of time, and it completely escaped me with you. May I escort you to your car?"

"Yes. Thank you. My car is with the valet."

"So is mine."

They were the last patrons in the clubhouse bar, and Lawrence walked her to the valet. While they waited for their cars, he gave her a light hug. On the way into the hug they kissed very briefly. He held on to her for a moment and stepped back, taking both of her hands in his as he moved slowly away. Their hands lost contact as her car pulled to a stop next to her and the valet stepped out, as though it had been planned and synchronized.

"Goodnight," he said.

"Goodnight."

Delores giggled as she drove away. Pedro had seen her on two dates in two weeks after not being at the club for so long. She was becoming a regular.

She thought about Lawrence. What a remarkable man. He was so genuine, confident and down to earth. He was direct with what he wanted, and he spoke his mind. He was ambitious, yet kind. It was obvious he cared about his kids and about being the best father he could. She was relieved to meet a man with solid family values, especially after the incident with Chandler. It was shocking that was less than a week ago.

She could hardly believe how free she felt. It was amazing. The feeling with Chandler was just to prepare her for this new level of enlightenment that had swept into her that evening. She had heard that things happen quickly when they do happen on the service, and she was beginning to believe it.

Delores went to sleep with a smile on her face.

18 DELORES – LAST FRIDAY

Delores returned from her ride to see a message from Lawrence.

'Good morning :)'

'Good morning!'

'I really enjoyed talking to you last night.'

'Me too.'

'It seems like next week is an eternity from now. I want to see you again sooner :)'

'Me too :)'

Delores had sent a smiley face, and it didn't come close to expressing the happiness she felt being interested in this man. It felt so reassuring to have a man interested in her and contacting her on a regular basis. The consistency of his messages, and having one to look forward to was making her giddy like a teenage girl. It was fun.

'Have a great day. I'll check in later.'

'Ok. Have a great day,' she replied.

At lunch Delores received another message.

'How is your day?'

'Hi. It's going well. I'm about to wrap up work for the week, and then see my dad in a little while. How is yours?'

'It's going well. I had a great week at work. I pick up the kids at 5 sharp. I'll grill for them.'

'That sounds nice. What do you like to grill?'

'Anything they will eat. They have a limited palate and I am not a cook.'

She did not respond.

'Chicken tonight.'

She did not respond.

'Maybe I can sneak out for sunset with you tomorrow.'

'Sneak out? Will the kids be okay?'

'They'll be fine with a movie. It will be a special treat for them to get a movie and for me to see you.'

'It will be a treat for me, too. I enjoy sunsets with you.'

'Perfect. I'll try to check in again later. Enjoy your afternoon with your dad :)'

':)'

When she got to the home to see Juergen, he was aware that a woman had entered the room. Sitting in the wingback chairs over tea, he spoke to her for the first time in several days.

"They told me."

"What is it that they told you?"

"You are my daughter. Are you?"

"Yes, Daddy. I am your daughter. I'm Delores."

"It is a pleasure to meet you. You are a pretty lady."

Juergen was slipping deeper into his disease. It didn't hurt as much today.

At 7 pm, Delores got a message from Lawrence.

'Just wanted to say hi. :)'

'Hi :)'

At 9 pm, another message arrived.

'Sweet dreams :)'

'To you, too. Goodnight.'

19 DELORES – LAST SATURDAY

After a long ride on Saturday morning, there was no message from Lawrence. It did not arrive until she was through with breakfast and reading the newspapers.

'Good morning :)'

'Hi :)'

'Really busy with the kids. Just wanted to say hi.'

'Have a great day'

'I always do with them. Still the best part will be sneaking away to see you.'

':)'

'7 pm at the shake shack across from Crystal Cove? We can walk down to the beach from there?'

'I will see you there at 7. Looking forward to the real version of your smile :)'

':)'

At 6:45 pm Delores was walking to her car dressed in dark, slim-fitting jeans, brown sandals with a 2" heel, and a loose camel sleeveless tank with a form-fitting black tank underneath. A black scarf with a subtle geometric pattern in blue finished her outfit. She felt wonderful and knew she looked radiant as well.

Delores made the quick drive to the shake shack in moments, arriving in time to walk to the north side of the property for some private reflection. She looked out at the calm ocean waters and the sun as it started sneaking away from her and the people scattered on the beach below.

At exactly 7 pm, Lawrence came up behind her and put his arms around her. It felt so natural. She tilted her head to the side and he kissed her temple.

"Hello. You are the most beautiful woman in the world."

She laughed.

"Thank you."

"I brought a blanket and bottle of wine. I figured we could have a glass while the sun goes down."

He picked up the basket he had brought along, and they started walking along the trail heading north toward the beach park. Delores noted his quiet confidence and thoughtfulness. He was sure of himself, calm, peaceful, and comfortable in who he was. There was no arrogance to this. He was wearing older jeans and a white t-shirt with brown leather sandals. He was so grounded. She felt like she could trust him with her life.

After they had walked a short distance, he took her hand in his.

"Do you mind if I hold your hand?"

"Not at all. I like it," she chuckled.

Again, conversation flowed very easily. They didn't talk about work or politics. Instead they just were. This was the same feeling of relief she had felt with Chandler to have companionship in the simplest form without any type of ranking, rating, or value assigned to it.

"This looks like a good spot to call ours for the night. Isn't this perfect? I love this view."

"Good choice. This reminds me of the view from my house only this is much closer."

"How far inland are you?"

"Oh, not far. My house is one of the closest to the coast. It was a lucky find. Pelican Point."

"That is lucky. How did you find it?"

"My father purchased it after his wife died. He needed a change of scenery from Lido Isle. He worked with the same broker he had used for decades. I have been staying at the coast house for the past couple years since he had not been managing well alone. I moved him last year when he needed extra care. It is important for me to be close. I'm sure you understand that with your kids. How did you find your house?"

"I found it online. Actually, I was lucky, too. It is quite tough to get a home that is move-in ready in Laguna Beach that is close to the beach, keeping in mind there are three kids who each need individual space. I actually found it the same hour it was listed, convinced the owners to give me the deal I wanted, and then take it off the market the same morning. They were a little hesitant because it is such a great spot and I responded so quickly. The first offer is always the best, though, and they realized I was a good candidate who would take care of the house."

Delores nodded.

"It works great for the kids. We are just up from the steps to the beach, and there is a separate yard. I can keep an eye on them when I'm grilling, and take them to the water when it's nice out. That's every day practically."

"Perfect. I appreciate how active you are with them."

"Thanks. I have the younger two kids until Wednesday. The older boy is going to a swim and water polo championship out of town. I am too busy to get time away from work, and the other two wouldn't sit still that long so I have them through the end of the trip. There is a sitter lined up for when I am at work, 9-5 all three days. Enough about them. I just want to look at you and drink you in with this glass of wine."

"It is another beautiful sunset."

"It is not as beautiful as you. Come here."

Delores let Lawrence pull her to him so that she was leaning back on him and they both looked out at the sunset. It felt so comfortable and natural. She was happy that he liked to cuddle. It had been a long time since she had been held. She thought it was something that she could get used to quickly.

The sun disappeared over the horizon, and the sky remained illuminated in shades of red, orange, and purple. The sky was a brilliant combination of colored clouds covering the pure blue. The water was glowing, and the sand was glimmering like a field of jewels.

Lawrence pulled her up and around just slightly so they were facing each other. He looked nervous, and she wondered if she looked as nervous as he did. She knew he was about to kiss her. It had been a long time since she had kissed anyone, and even longer since she felt so comfortable in the arms of a man.

She liked him. She wanted him to kiss her.

Neither said a word as they stared into each other's eyes.

"I really like you," he said.

"I like you, too. It is refreshing to like someone."

He nodded and inched forward to kiss her. She stared to lean in, no longer nervous to return his kiss. He playfully dodged her lips and touched his nose to hers, gently teasing hers. She gasped and smiled. She was so excited.

He smiled and pressed his lips gently to hers. She kissed him back softly. It was a sensual kiss.

After a moment, Lawrence pulled away.

"My opinion of the service has just gone up a notch," he said. "Make that many notches."

She laughed heartily.

"Definitely. I had no expectations. This was a treat. You are a treat."

He kissed her again. This time there was a well of passion that she felt coursing through her. She moaned a little moan of pleasure, and he slowly pulled away.

"I have two kids to tend to. I wish I could stay with you. This is perfect."

"Kissing you is perfect."

He kissed her briefly, and then pulled away slowly. He helped her up and folded the blanket. He corked the wine bottle, and returned everything to the basket. Instead of holding hands he put his arm around her as they walked up the path back to the shake shack and their cars.

Delores led him to her car, where he wrapped his arms around her once more. He kissed her forehead, and stepped back as she got into the driver's seat and started the car. He closed the door for her and stepped backward a couple paces. He waved as she exited the parking lot.

Again, Delores was swooning over his kind, warm, gentle manner. She wondered how any woman had let a man like this go, especially after 23 years.

She climbed into bed at 10 pm, and a message appeared from Lawrence just then.

'Sweet dreams, beautiful :)'

'Goodnight :)'

Delores fell asleep with a big smile on her face and fell quickly into sweet dreams.

20 DELORES – SUNDAY

Delores took the morning off from biking. She stayed in bed and enjoyed the peace and quiet with thoughts of Lawrence. After some time, she grew restless and retreated to the patio for breakfast and to read the newspaper.

It was 9:30 when she received the first text message from Lawrence.

'Good morning :)'

'Hi :)'

'I woke up thinking about you.'

'Me too.'

'What does your week look like? I want to see you.'

'My friend Valerie is visiting from Martha's Vineyard. I'll spend a couple days with her at Balboa Bay Club. Great for her kids and we get to talk during their activities.'

'That's great you keep friendships across the country.'

'Valerie and I have been friends for 30 years. I'm glad to have time with her. When are you available?'

'I have the kids through Wednesday. I want to see you.'

'Ok, let me know when.'

'I miss you.'

'I miss you, too.'

'I'll check in later. Have a wonderful day, Delores!'

That afternoon following the visit with her father, she received another message.

'Just wanted to say hi :)'

'Hi :) How is your day?'

'Stressful at best.'

'Do you want to talk about it?'

'No. It's just that the sitter canceled and I need to figure out something for the kids this week. Nobody is available at short notice.'

'Can I help?'

'Not unless you are a sitter...'

'Not exactly.'

'Thanks anyway :)'

'Best wishes. I hope it works out that you don't need to take off work.'

'Thanks. Taking off is not an option. Big meetings this week. I don't normally handle sitters.'

Delores thought a moment. It sounded like he was really in a tough situation and she easily could help.

'Well, I'm sure they can come along to Balboa Bay Club.'

'They're 8 and 11. Not exactly an easy pair.'

'Valerie's kid are enrolled in day activities. I'll have your kids added.'

'What if they are full?'

'Between Valerie and me, I assure you your kids will have spots. Guaranteed.'

'That would be amazing. You are amazing. I have been sweating this all day! How do I pay for them?'

'That won't be necessary. Just bring them by at 8:30. What are their names and ages?'

'Christian, 11. Annabelle, 8. To the club?'

'Yes.'

'Thank you. This is delicate, of course, because they don't know that I am dating. They are still dealing with things in their own little people way.'

'I will be discreet. There is nothing to worry about. They will be in activities all day. They'll love it.'

'Not as much as I will. You are wonderful.'

'You just need to sign a waiver when you get there. They'll be under Valerie Vanderbilt.'

'You are amazing. Then I can see you, too, when I drop them off and pick them up :)'

'You caught my ulterior motive in this, then...'

'Delores, you are amazing. How did I get so lucky as to find you?'

'I could ask, too... Where did you come from?'

'lol :) Laguna Beach. I would love to give you a giant hug and kiss right now.'

'I'll see you at 8:30, then.'

'Yes, I'll check in before that, though :)'

At sunset, Delores looked out over the Pacific Ocean. She had just played fetch with her beloved dogs, and they were enjoying their dinner in their dining area now. She was happy that she could help Lawrence. He was such a warm and kind man. She was slipping easily into the pattern of texting him several times a day. She realized they had never spoken on the phone. That was fine for her. It was certainly different and oddly efficient. She mainly was flattered that he got in touch. He was thinking of her, and their feelings were mutual.

It was exciting to think of seeing him in the morning with his kids. They looked so precious in the photos he had posted online. What would it be like to have kids? Even though she would not be interacting with them, it would be interesting to be in charge of children. Would she be a good stepmother? Would she be a good mother? It was a very tough question for her to consider. The concept was absolutely foreign. She only had dealt with children a few steps removed. Nelda was the one raising her dogs as well. This was a lot to absorb.

At 9:30 pm, Lawrence texted.
'Good night. I am so excited to see you in the morning :)'
'Sweet dreams, Lawrence :)'
'You are an angel. Big hug'

21 MAIZIE – SUNDAY

Maizie was getting good at the new system. The pink zone turned out to be too generous, and it kept shrinking. The red zone took up most of the map. She was so happy that she hadn't had to waste her time driving around through the neighborhoods that made up the pink zone. The men consistently were revealing traits that clearly were inconsistent with wealth. They made it easy for her to reject them quickly and continue the search.

She still had a hard time believing how slow many of the men were to pursue. If she had looked at half their profiles on the East Coast, all of them would have contacted her. Not here. And she saw who her competition was on a daily basis. She was far hotter than them. She was smarter. Her profile was written with the type of marketing expertise that most people would kill to have.

Maybe she was scaring them. Her confidence and beauty must have been overwhelming them. It was the land of men raised by single mothers. Perhaps that was part of it.

Most of her matches were either in the wrong color zone or extremely boring. There was not a lot in between. She was not finding much individuality. It was difficult to find a man who would be an intelligent partner, yet who would dedicate himself to her entirely when not making the money she required to stay in the relationship.

She never had thought of herself as a gold-digger. Everywhere else she had lived, there had been a clear path to the upper class lifestyle for that area. In Laguna Beach, though, that was not possible without an external boost. She didn't like that she couldn't just have an oceanfront home.

She wanted her own media company. Partnering with the photographer she had met in Fiji would be incredible. There just was no way to do that without someone supporting her. She wanted to have the luxury to do as she chose, and not be forced to follow a career path defined by someone else. She was sick of waiting.

Maizie opened the service site on her computer, and checked out her new matches using the system. First, she sorted based on the map. Then she looked at the men who had requested communication. Finally, she opened the profiles of the new matches who were in the green zone. Today there were only two.

Steven from Newport Beach, 49
Real Estate / Investments
I'm looking for a partner with an easy smile - a positive outlook, good quick sense of humor, and laughing eyes. A good listener, who can also honestly express her thoughts well.

While simple, Steven was clear. It sounded like he was looking for a trophy wife who would direct him. That was actually perfect. He needed to look good and it seemed he would accept feedback and be teachable. He may be a great tool. Unless he owned half the coast he was a purely temporary man. His connections would be a fast track for her. She sent him a smile. She smiled to herself. This was perfect. He was looking for someone who would charm his clients. He would melt with her in front of him.

Lawrence from Laguna Beach, 44
Managing Director
I was in a 23 year relationship that started when I was in college, and now I am looking for a successful independent new partner with similar interests to share in the next phase of my life. My ideal partner will understand that I am an excellent father who is actively involved in my kids' daily lives. It would be refreshing to know a woman can help make me the man I was meant to be and raise me up. Life is too short for the alternative (hence my marriage is over). I'm doing my best, and always do. It's better with a partner. I picture sharing a bottle of wine on a romantic evening, and bringing a smile to each other's faces.

This one was interesting. He obviously had a big heart and wanted to be with someone. Lawrence sounded lonely, and slightly desperate to share himself. It was odd that he also was a managing director. The details of his profile revealed a career with a Wall Street company. He was a sheep in a lion's world. He seemed so compassionate, and to be involved in finance she expected there was another side to him. Interesting. He did live in Laguna Beach, and with the kids he would have to be in a larger place than she was. Reading the rest of his profile, he came across as intelligent, clean-cut, and extremely stable. He wanted companionship, and was not pathetic. Still, he got the sympathy vote. She did not send a message or a smile. If he wanted to go for it, then it was up to him.

Maizie closed the service site and texted Drew.
'Good night'
As always, he responded immediately.
'Good night, gorgeous. I can't wait to see you.'
':) I'll see you tomorrow evening :)'
She was not excited to see him. She was excited about the evening he had planned. They were having dinner prepared by a private chef on an ocean side cliff in South Laguna Beach. This was a first for her. It seemed like something she could get used to fast. It was easy to drop breadcrumbs for Drew.

She had gotten him away from communicating through the service site last week, but only after he had worked hard to feel like they were exclusive. She saw he had not been active on the site since then. The last thing she wanted was for him to see that she was going on the site regularly. It was unfortunate that the date of her last activity was shown. Otherwise she could have her cell phone uninterrupted by texts from these men who each thought he was her only beau.

Aside from that, she wanted her matches off the site. She wanted them in the habit of communicating only with her rather than looking at other matches. She did not want her attention to go to a match's head and cause him to think he could play the field with her in tow. That is not how it worked. This way she was free to have many men thinking that she was theirs.

Idiots.

22 DELORES – MONDAY

Delores returned from a short ride early on Monday morning so she could prepare for her big day as step-mother-in-training. Well, perhaps it was more like step-mother-in-observation or step-mother-in-contemplation. All she was doing was meeting the children that may one day become her stepchildren. It was a first.

She was not quite certain what to wear. She decided on a conservative white and tan bikini for the pool, and a lightweight sleeveless cotton dress in tan and pink for the rest of the day. Her new pink and tan sandals matched perfectly. She had a white linen cover-up and a wide-brimmed woven hat with white piping and accents. Delores again was grateful for the newly reorganized closet.

She picked up her phone on the way down to the patio for breakfast at 7:15. At 6:30 a message had arrived from Lawrence.

'Good morning :) Big hug and kiss :)'

'I'm looking forward for the real thing. The kids are confirmed under Valerie Vanderbilt.'

'Beautiful.'

A few minutes later, another message.

'You are beautiful. See you soon. Where can I see just you?'

'You can meet Valerie and me in the lobby. Low-key introductions. You two can check in kids, and I will meet you at the marina.'

'You are amazing :)'

Delores was delighted that Lawrence was thinking about her and continued to text each morning. She was happy to be doing him a favor today, and even happier that she would get to see him the next three days while he had his kids. The fact that he was open to her suggestion for the marina meeting impressed her. It would be brief, yes, and it also would be a reminder of what she would have to herself soon. It was obvious that it would be too soon to go out with him while he had the kids.

Another great advantage to him bringing the kids to Balboa Bay Club is her good friend Valerie could meet him and give Delores her opinion. After Chandler, she was open to feedback from friends so such complications could be avoided.

Balboa Bay Club was the oldest private club in Newport Beach. The resort included a pool, fitness area, suites, an expansive beach along Newport Bay, and the best youth activity program in the area. It was stately and elegant, and the admission criteria were quite selective. Delores and Valerie had been going to the club since they were little girls. They had learned to swim and sail during summers in the day program. Valerie was adamant that her daughters have the same experience.

At 8:25, Delores and Valerie were in the lobby with her three blonde girls: Hazel, 12, Hilda, 11, and Heather, 7. Lawrence and his smooth-skinned, tanned, brunette children greeted them. Their hair appeared freshly cut and was combed neatly. They were clothed in pressed designer outfits and flip-flops. Each child had a small backpack with beach gear, sneakers, and a change of clothes. She admired his organization. It would not be difficult for them to join the youth activities today.

Lawrence was wearing black wool slacks, a blue dress shirt that matched the face of his Rolex, and a pink tie patterned with small blue seashells. His shoes were polished, and his black close-cropped hair was combed impeccably. He stood tall at 6'1", and looked better than he had on the other two occasions. This was the first time she was seeing him before his day started, and it was exciting. Appearance and grooming obviously were important to him. He was devilishly handsome, yet the subtle vulnerability was present.

Lawrence introduced her as Miss Delores, and explained they were to behave during their activities and obey both her and Miss Valerie during any breaks. They shook her hand and politely followed Valerie and Lawrence to registration.

Delores was glad to watch the process for a few moments and she could tell that Valerie approved. In fact, as she slipped away to the marina at the edge of the resort to meet Lawrence, she was certain that her friend was flirting with her newfound man. Delores smiled.

This was a new experience. Most of her relationships, having been with married men, did not involve getting together with her friends. They especially did not include getting together with his friends or family. She was happier still that Valerie could give an assessment before she knew there was a budding romance between Delores and Lawrence. She was looking forward to telling Valerie when she met her for breakfast at 9:00.

Lawrence stepped out to the marina, and they embraced. He leaned down to give her a tender kiss and held it for several minutes, pulling her closer and closer as they kissed. Her smile grew so large it was difficult to kiss him, and she laughed when they pulled away.

"The only difficult thing about kissing you is that my smile is so big when I'm in your arms," she confessed.

"I know what you mean. I have been looking forward to having you in my arms since Saturday night."

"I am happy I could see you and help. Your kids are adorable."

"They had best behave today. I'll pick them up at 5 o'clock sharp. We'll have to wait until morning to sneak another kiss, though. Is that okay?"

He kissed her briefly and stepped back.

"Did I already tell you that you look beautiful in that dress?"

She smiled.

"Thank you. No, you hadn't."

"You do. You're amazing. How did I get so lucky?"

She giggled.

"I'll check in later."

Moments later, Delores joined Valerie in the dining room.

"Delores, who is that man? He is so handsome! If I didn't know better I would say he is your new boyfriend! Where did he come from?"

Delores laughed while answering her friend, "Laguna Beach."

"What is the story with him?"

"First, tell me what you think!"

"I already did. He is sharp. He is perfect, and his kids are perfect. He is so warm and kind, and his kids have better manners than most adults. Seriously, who is he? He obviously is successful, and he is completely taken by you. What are you hiding? Is he single?"

"You think he is taken by me... Why do you say that?"

"Delores, in his mind he was practically hammering himself into the marble floor to keep from throwing himself at you. The man has eyes for you. Believe me."

"I'm glad you say that. We went out a couple times last week, and he was in a bind with childcare this week. His ex-wife has their oldest son on a trip for a team sporting event, and his sitter canceled yesterday. He couldn't find a replacement sitter, so I offered to put them here while we visit. I thought I could catch a glimpse of his paternal side and see what his kids are like without having to interact with them. It works out perfectly."

"You are sly! How did you meet him?"

Delores was embarrassed to answer.

"You won't believe this. I met him online."

"What? Online? That's outrageous! When did you go online?"

"Oh, this is complicated. I promise I'll tell you more. Isn't Lawrence nice, though?"

"Delores, of course he is nice. He wants to sleep with you. Men aren't just nice. They are nice because they want something. Believe me. And I cannot believe you are using an online matching service to find dates! This has scandal written all over it! Tell me more!"

Delores confessed the Chandler debacle. She and Valerie spent the day laughing, catching up, and stealing occasional glances at the children. The children also were enjoying their activities. It was perfect.

After lunch and before Delores left to see her father, the ladies decided to ignore the old wives' tale and got into the swimming pool with full stomachs. When she got out of the pool there was a message from Lawrence.

'Just wanted to say hi :)'

While she was waiting for the valet to get her car, she responded.

'Hope your day is going well. The kids are having a great time.'

'I miss you.'

'I miss you, too.'

It was odd. She actually did miss him. She was not used to missing people. Where was this coming from? She realized she was falling for this man. He hadn't even taken her to dinner!

That night at 9:15, she received a message from Lawrence.

'Thank you so much. The kids are so happy, and they went to bed on time like angels.'

'My pleasure.'

'Good night, beautiful :)'

'Good night'

'I am excited to see you in the morning. Same time and place?'

'Yes :) Sweet dreams'

For the fifth night in a row, Delores fell asleep with a smile on her face.

23 MAIZIE – MONDAY

Maizie had an early evening workout session at the private gym so that she could get ready to meet Drew for dinner at 7 pm. She was not comfortable having him pick her up at her home. Sure it was respectable. It was Laguna Beach. However, the fact it was a multi-unit property set among other multi-unit properties did not give the right image. She wanted to be on par with Drew for as long as possible so he didn't think he had the advantage of wealth as a given. She wanted the extravagant treatment to continue and only reveal the limitations of her five-figure income after fine excursions were a habit.

She had found another new dress at work today that was perfectly beach casual or dressy. It was a flowing tan and blue print asymmetric dress that stopped mid-thigh. It was accessorized with a white belt, and Maizie chose blue sandals and a necklace made of large blue stones. Her hair required only a quick brushing, and her makeup was minimal so she would have a natural look that coordinated with the cliff side setting.

With a little extra time before she had to leave, she decided to do the daily sorting on the dating service. To her surprise, there was a message received at 6:20 am from Lawrence, whose profile she had viewed, and not from Steven, to whom she had sent a smile. Steven had viewed her profile at lunchtime, and had not responded. These California men were such a puzzle. She had been certain she would have that one.

She responded to Lawrence's questions and sent a set of her own to him. This process was so lame. She was nearly ready to explore other options.

Before she could get through all the sorting it was time to go. She always liked to be early to get her bearings in new places, and this definitely was no exception.

Dinner was incredible, and Maizie savored every morsel of her soup, steak, salt-crusted fish, sauteed vegetables, and vanilla bean creme brulee with brandied berry compote. The wine was exquisite. Drew's taste in wine continued to impress her. She did not have to ask for anything. Her wishes were catered before she knew of them. This was the type of treatment she wanted every day. Drew would remain as long as he continued to please her like this.

Drew expected a real kiss after dinner. She would not give him one. He had tried to kiss her in the lobby before dinner, and she wouldn't let him. She was glad he was getting assertive, and gladder that she had the control of not giving in to his desires. He had a few more dates to go before getting physical. Instead she gave him several light kisses, touched him, teased him, and leaned over so he could catch a glimpse of her bare breasts under her dress. It was fun to play with him visually. That would be enough.

When Maizie returned home at 10 pm, she returned to the service site to finish her sorting and communication. There was another message from Lawrence. She responded to his character trait lists with her own, and then continued to groom the page that contained her matches. She was about to close her computer for the night when another message came from Lawrence. He wanted to skip the rest of the standard steps and communicate by messages. She accepted his request and dismissed the pop-up with the safety tips that she had memorized.

His message was simple.

'Your profile made me smile. Rare to find someone from Laguna Beach, isn't it?'

'Hi Lawrence. Thank you.'

She didn't want to elaborate on her matches. He did not need to know anything about what kind of matches she got, where they lived, or what she did with them.

'Have you lived in LB for a long time?'

'I just moved here from the East Coast this year.'

'LB is a special place. Where in LB do you live?'

She didn't feel like engaging in a long conversation with this lonely man so late at night, especially on the first day of communication. He seemed to be really lonely and to want someone to talk to.

'I love it. I live downtown. I have an early morning. Goodnight.'

'Ok. I'll write more tomorrow. Goodnight.'

24 DELORES – TUESDAY

At 6:45, there was a message from Lawrence.
'Good morning. How was your bike ride?'
'Hi. Great. It's my favorite way to start the day.'
'Mine is seeing you :) Big hug and kisses
'Big hug and kiss back.'

They all met in the lobby again, and Valerie took the kids to check in while Lawrence and Delores stepped out to the marina. She was happy to have an extra ten minutes with him. He was even sexier today with gray pants and a black button down shirt with a blue and gray paisley print tie.

They embraced once outside, and kissed. Today the kiss was even more passionate. He pulled her closer and moaned lightly as she worked her hands down to his butt and squeezed lightly. She was so attracted to him.

He pulled back from the kiss, still holding her tightly.

"I missed you. I can't wait to have you all to myself. You're so beautiful."

"I missed you, too." Again she was surprised that she really did miss him when she was waiting to see him again.

"When I text you, there is so much more I want to say. I don't want to seem desperate or anything. It's just that I feel such a connection with you, Delores. I'm not used to being so comfortable around people, and you really put me at ease. There is no word for what I feel for you. It's so intense. A new word has to be invented to describe this feeling."

"I know what you mean. I don't know how this has happened so quickly. I have heard that when things happen through this service they happen fast. That is being proven true here. I'm so attracted to you in every

133

way."

He kissed her again.

"I want to see you alone," he breathed.

"Me, too. Where did you come from?"

"And how did I get so lucky? That can be our joke," he said as he pulled back and smiled at her.

"I'll check in later. Text me if the kids don't behave."

He kissed her again before stepping back and retreating to the lobby.

The day continued smoothly. Valerie and Delores each had calls and business to tend to, so they used the executive center for most of the morning and only met for lunch. The friendship was flexible, and they both knew it was better to mix the social time with work so no resentments would form.

"You are absolutely smitten with this fellow, aren't you?"

"Yes, I am."

"What do you like most about him?"

"He is consistent, and he always follows through with what he says he is going to do. I feel like he is trustworthy. It is quite natural to be with him. He's excited to see me, and I'm excited to see him. He sends me messages throughout the day, and I feel like I'm being courted. I get to feel like a girl again instead of a hard-pressing executive or fear-stricken daughter. We will have time alone soon, and I'm really looking forward to being with him."

"He certainly does seem perfect. Have you asked about his divorce? It really is a big deal with kids that age. Don't sleep with him yet. You need to know more about who he is first. You need to know his intentions and make sure he is not just sampling the goods. I want you to have the real deal, and he needs to prove to you that he is."

"Oh, I know. I'll know when it's right."

"Be careful. You're smitten right now."

Just then a text came in.

'Hi gorgeous. Just wanted to let you know I'm thinking of you.'

"See? This is such a treat! Valerie, I didn't realize how lonely I was until a few weeks ago. This man is a gift!"

"Just be careful, Delores. He seems perfect now, and I just want to make sure you're not jumping in too fast."

"I know. I appreciate your concern."

"You have a lot of emotional activity going on now. Just please be careful not to put too much energy on this man until you are sure who he is. I want to see you happy, and I sincerely hope he can contribute to you being happy. You're absolutely radiant now."

"Thank you. I love you, Valerie."

Delores was grateful for her friendship with Valerie. As with Wendy, they did not need to speak regularly in order to pick up on what was going on in their lives.

She took Valerie's advice for what it was and was sure she could trust her intuition when it came to Lawrence. It was all so natural.

At 9:15 pm, she received a text from Lawrence. It was like clockwork.
'Goodnight beautiful :)'
'Sweet dreams :)'

25 MAIZIE –TUESDAY

Maizie sat down for her match filtering at 9 pm. There were no new matches who had made it to the green zone. The pink zone had the most candidates. The red zone also had no matches. She wondered if the matching was smart enough to see whom she was closing and would start giving her more relevant matches at some point. Her routine was so consistent, and there were still the same types of matches delivered. She assumed there just were not a lot of potential matches in the green zone. Maybe they used another service. She would look into that. Regardless, she still had messages from her matches in the green zone.

Lawrence had written. Steven had not.

'Hi Maizie, I get coffee downtown every morning (when I find parking, that is). Maybe we can meet for coffee one of these days?'

'Sure. Sounds good to me. I can just walk there :)'

'Great. Does Saturday morning work for you?'

'Yes. I have some time Saturday.'

'Just name the time and place and I'll be there :)'

Maizie decided to leave him hanging a day. No point in appearing too eager. There was no protocol for the time frame in which she had to respond to him.

26 DELORES –WEDNESDAY

At 6:45, there was a message from Lawrence.

'Good morning :) How was your bike ride?'

Delores loved that he sent it at 6:45 even though she didn't always respond right away. Whenever she texted him, though, he responded immediately. She didn't understand how he could type fast enough to get the messages back to her so quickly.

'Hi. It was nice. Climbed a big hill today. That's always fun.'

'I'll take your word for it and keep my feet on the ground :) See you at 8:30?'

'I can't wait.'

'Big hug and kiss :)'

Again, they met at the marina after the kids joined Valerie in the lobby. He was wearing a chocolate brown suit with a pale blue shirt. His tie was dark blue with small white waves in a loose pattern.

"Hello, beautiful."

"Good morning. You are a handsome devil."

"And you look more amazing every time I see you. It's so good for me to be right here. Being with you I don't want to leave you."

He pulled her close and they kissed. It was tender and passionate. She was excited as their bodies pressed together. He had such a firm body. She was excited to see more of it.

"It's not enough to say I'm thinking of you all the time. I am so happy that I met you, Lawrence."

"I know. It feels like fate." He kissed her. "Can I take you out tomorrow? The kids are getting picked up at 8 pm tonight, and then I'm free."

"Oh, no! I have to fly to Nashville tomorrow for a meeting. I'll be back Saturday, though."

"That is a quick trip! I'm glad, though, because I don't know if I could wait much longer to hold you in my arms again. I want to have you all to myself."

He kissed her again. It was a hungry kiss. It was the kind of kiss that expressed wanting more. She put all she had into the kiss, and they both let out small sighs of pleasure as their bodies pressed together through all those layers of clothing. Now she was extremely excited to be with him when she returned.

Delores and Valerie had another morning together, and mostly relaxed beside the pool. The combination of relaxing with her friend and daydreaming about Lawrence left Delores less alert than normal. Though it seemed like only an hour had passed, she realized it was nearly 2 pm, and she rushed off to see her father. While waiting for her car from valet, she noticed a second message from Lawrence.

'I want to come early and sneak a kiss. Can you meet me at the marina at 4:45?'

'Yes :)'

At 4:45 sharp Lawrence arrived at to the marina and took Delores in his arms, holding her tight.

"I just had to hold you again before you leave town."

Her heart rate increased with the warmth from this man. She felt so good and so cherished. She felt loved.

"I'm going to miss you."

"I miss you already, Delores. We are meant to be together. This is fate."

He kissed her again, and she gave in entirely.

At 9:15 her phone buzzed.

'Are you packed?'

Nelda's assistant had packed for her the previous day.

'Yes. Ready to go.'

'Big hug and kiss :)'

'Many kisses to you, Lawrence'

27 MAIZIE – WEDNESDAY

Her workout was fabulous. Not only had she burned more calories and done more repetitions of some new weight training exercises, she also had gotten information from Rick about an online matching service that was a notch up from the one she was using. It was aimed solely at millionaires. There still would be a zone filtering system. It would eliminate a lot of other questions, though. These would be men who knew how to make money. It would not be necessary to network through multiple stages to get to the right level financially.

Maizie marveled at how much her taste had changed from her juvenile interest in Jared a month ago to understanding what it really would take to get to the next level in her life with a real man. Before investigating the new site, she went through the filtering process on her current matches. There were none who made the green zone.

There was another message from Lawrence.

'How was your day?'

'Good. Yours? I can meet you at 9:30 am Saturday at the corner cafe on Broadway.'

He actually replied right away.

'Perfect. I'll be sitting at the counter outside looking over the water.'

'I'll see you then.'

'You can text me at 949-555-2345 if anything changes.'

Maizie again decided to ignore his message.

She pulled up the site her trainer had told her about, and created a profile for millionaires to see. This would speed up the process certainly. The demands of her new job were starting to annoy her, and the sooner she could get out on her own with her independent media company the better.

She was determined to be in one of the large homes that dotted the coast by the same time the next year. Even better, she wanted her name to be on the title.

28 DELORES –THURSDAY

At 6:45, there was a message from Lawrence.

'Good morning. Have a safe flight. I miss you :)'

He was like clockwork.

'Thanks. I miss you, too.'

She again was surprised that she actually did miss him. He made her feel so good. She liked letting him cherish her. She was glad her serious and mundane days now also included cheerful messages from him. She was flattered that this handsome, successful man was thinking of her enough to take a break from his day and send them.

Chloe had prepared similar transportation and accommodation arrangements for this trip to Nashville. Delores was to meet with two organizations for two of her three clients, and then follow up in person with each of the clients. The first meeting was that night for dinner, and the second was on Friday morning. Friday she had lunch with Birdie at Capital Grill and dinner with Bunny at the country club. Saturday morning she would meet Dolly at the same country club for breakfast before getting on the private jet back to California.

She expected only one more trip before all of the programs for the new clients were in place. She was pleased with the efficiency with which she had handled these deals. Lawrence was making her so happy. The work flew past quicker than it ever had. She had heard that love made that happen. It was beginning to look like that was the case with him.

'Delores I'm thinking of you, and only you.'

That was a wonderful message to get from Lawrence before dinner.

She was glowing as she headed into her meeting that night.

':) Big hug.'

'Good night. I'll dream of you :)'

How thoughtful of him to send her a message that would arrive at 9:15 in her time zone!

'Sweet dreams, Lawrence.'

Delores enjoyed the habit of going to bed with a smile on her face and in her heart.

29 MAIZIE – THURSDAY

Maizie was trying to get used to the new site, and it was rather annoying. Names were not given, and instead it was user names. That seemed immature for a millionaire-focused site. Perhaps people were trying to protect their identities. Pictures made that impossible unless they were outdated or of someone else, which many were. The matching criteria were not intuitive, and she was certain that her own non-millionaire status seeking millionaire was placing a limit on how many qualified matches she received. The ones she did get were nowhere close to the green zone.

For the amount the site was charging, she was glad there was someone in customer service whose real name and email address were provided. She sent a note to the administrator expressing her frustration and insisted a mistake had been made in registration. She insisted her own status must have been set to non-millionaire by mistake, and that it must be changed at once or she would cancel the subscription.

So far it seemed this was a service for patient people and for people who were okay moving across the country for the sake of a fortune. That was not what she wanted. She wanted to stay where she was and have the money come to her. Hmmm. Actually it would not be awful if the man stayed far away and maintained a separate home for them in coastal Orange County. In fact, that may be negotiable. She could have all that she wanted and not have to share the house with him. She did not want someone to keep her company. Still, there was a certain degree of comfort in seeing regularly the degree to which she controlled her men. He had to be local.

Maizie closed the new millionaire site and switched back to her old service. Again no new matches made it to the green zone. And again, there was a message from Lawrence.

'Hi Maizie, just wondered if you could meet for a drink tonight or tomorrow in lieu of coffee Saturday?'

It was 7:15, and he had just sent the message. She figured there was nothing to lose meeting him for a drink. The quicker she could filter the better.

'Lawrence, I'm busy tomorrow night. I can meet you tonight at 8:30.'

He responded right away. He always did.

'Do you know where the Sand and Sea is in Laguna Beach? There is a great patio with cozy seating. I'll see you there at 8:30. I can't wait.'

She thought he must be very lonely. He would have her sympathy if she cared that much. She did not care so he did not get it.

'Ok. I'm looking forward to meeting you.'

Whatever.

'Text me if anything changes: 949-555-2345.'

He sure seemed nervous about getting stood up for their coffee and drink dates. She was not about to give him her number. There was a ways to go yet. She had to hook him first.

Maizie chose the same blue dress she had worn to Mastro's and Fleming's. She knew she was sexy. Lawrence would be flattered to go from lonely to sharing an evening with her looking all exotic. She hoped he was not a waste of time, and was eager to know if he was worth further communication.

Arriving at the Sand and Sea, she was impressed with the casual elegance of the resort. It was simple and clean, and every detail was of high quality without being pretentious. She made her way to the patio lounge and was greeted by the incredibly handsome Lawrence. He looked a good 20 pounds lighter than in the pictures. He was wearing dark jeans with intentionally weathered areas on the thighs, and his button down black shirt remained un-tucked. His shoes were fine black Italian loafers, and he was wearing a Rolex with a beautiful blue face and tasteful sprinkling of diamonds. His dark hair was combed neatly in a classic clean-cut style, and its darkness accentuated the green of his eyes. They sparkled and were very inviting.

His demeanor was entirely disarming. Immediately, her guard was down. She could do nothing to get it back if she wasn't careful. She was melting into his eyes. He was so handsome. She was quickly uncomfortable with the effect he had on her. It was bizarre.

"Hello," he said and put out his hand for her to shake.

Maizie's smile grew as she stretched out her hand to shake his. He obviously was not used to dating. Who shook hands anymore? That was so formal. He was absolutely adorable. She was quickly at ease and assured that she was, in fact, the one with the power.

"Hi."

"You look stunning."

"Thank you."

The hostess led them to a pair of chairs that was set up at an angle to each other. A heater was on one side and a glass railing protected them from the ocean breeze while providing a view to the waves, illuminated by large spotlights as they crashed onto the sand below. She loved absorbing the power of the ocean. It made her feel invincible.

Once seated they had privacy, and it felt like a home. She wanted a balcony like this. She wanted more of this man, too. He would not have to be lonely for long. He was by far the best match yet. She would have him eating out of her hand in no time.

"I'm so glad you were able to come out tonight. My plans canceled at the last minute. I try to take advantage whenever I have time to meet a special lady like you."

"It worked out really well. I had just returned from dinner, and I have a lot to celebrate today."

"Why is that?"

She smiled. He didn't need to know she was celebrating meeting him.

"I'll tell you soon enough. Tell me more about you. How long have you lived in Laguna Beach?"

"I found my home in Laguna two years ago after my marriage was over. I love it. It is a very special place. You just moved here this year?"

"Yes. I love it, too. I had never been here, and fell in love with it on the first visit."

"I know the feeling. Sometimes it is like that. When it is meant to be, it just happens. That's with all things," he responded and winked. "Do you think you'll stay around long term?"

"Absolutely. I grow more attached every day."

The conversation continued with ease. She was completely open and still flirtatious. This was not a waste of time. His warmth and wealth were intoxicating. And he was so incredibly sexy. Aside from the initial introduction she felt entirely in control.

"Have you been using the service for a long time?" he asked.

"I've used it in the past, and it just seemed like a natural way to meet people being new in town." That wasn't exactly a lie. "What about you?"

"For me it has been off and on. I meet a lot of fascinating women, and still there isn't a lot of potential for a relationship. You have to watch out. There are a lot of people using the service who have ulterior motives."

"Are you trying to protect me?"

"No. I'm just sharing my experience. I have had to be careful. Very careful. Trust is an interesting thing. I work with people for a living and I am an expert in email marketing, so I can usually tell within a few messages or texts what the character of a match is. That helps a lot. Some people are just out for something other than they say they are. It's one thing to put that on their profiles, and another in person. Do you know what I mean? This area is especially challenging because there is so much wealth and temptation."

Maizie nodded.

"I agree. What are you looking for?"

Lawrence smiled.

"I like confident, beautiful women. I believe in strong relationships and open communication. I am not as interested in superficial things, or things that don't last like looks, sex, and material possessions defining a relationship. Any of those things come and go. To me it is the values that matter. That is what lasts. I want a partner to share my life with, and who understands we will have some variation in how we perceive each other. I believe in commitment, and in working through things together. I believe in marriage. I am a family guy 100%. I would have a hard time with someone who didn't like kids or who did not want kids. I have three and they are not going anywhere. And I still have time away from them, so it potentially is the best of both worlds."

"You're very certain of that. I think that is sexy."

"I am also very certain that I want to kiss you right now."

He leaned over and kissed her, his lips soft and gentle. It was not sexual or threatening. It was casual affection. She knew he couldn't help himself.

She liked it. This was not a waste of time. She was thrilled with his potential.

"My opinion of the service just went up a notch. Your lips are amazing," he said.

"Where did you come from?"

Lawrence laughed. "Laguna Beach."

The conversation went on, and it was interspersed with the same small kisses. She felt like the only woman on the planet, and he was eating right out of her hand.

"I know you have plans tomorrow night. Would you still like to go for coffee on Saturday? I really want to see you again."

"9:30 at the corner cafe is still on my calendar."

"I don't want to leave you right now, but it is getting to be that time. Can I walk you to your car?"

"If you insist."

He walked her to her Mini Cooper, and gave her a hug with another light kiss. She liked that he was too nervous to actually make out with her, and also that he was confident enough to express his interest with small kisses.

"Good night," he said. He closed the door after she climbed into her car and waved as she drove away.

30 DELORES – FRIDAY

At 8:45 am, there was a message from Lawrence. She did not blame him for sending it later. He would have had to wake up extremely early to sent it to her at 6:45 in Nashville.

'Good morning beautiful :)'

Before she could respond, another message arrived.

'Oh, no! I hope you will forgive me....'

She was curious what he was talking about.

'What do you mean?'

'We met a week ago yesterday. I forgot to mention it. It seems like so much longer! It is just so natural:)'

'I know. I feel so comfortable with you.'

'Same here. It must be fate. Happy one week anniversary :) Big hug'

Delores went through her day with a silly smile on her face, and everything flowed easily. Even meeting with Birdie went smoothly. The woman truly was difficult, and all of her attempts to penetrate Delores's professional veneer failed. Delores thought she had weathered all the meetings with grace and dignity, and all parties involved had walked away feeling confident with what would come from the partnerships. She was certain the money would be handled honestly.

Friday night at 9:30, she received a message from Lawrence.

'Good night. I can't wait to see you when you get back tomorrow. We can celebrate one week :) What time?'

'7 pm. I am excited to see you. Sweet dreams :)'

'Big hug'

31 MAIZIE – FRIDAY

Maizie didn't actually have plans on Friday night. She was relieved to spend some time by herself for a change. She wanted to do some journaling after she checked the sites. She decided to start with what she knew and logged into the old site. There were no new green zone matches. Two messages from Lawrence had been received, the first at 6:45 am and the second at 5:00 pm.

'Good morning. I really enjoyed meeting you last night. I'm looking forward to seeing you tomorrow and getting to know you better. Have a wonderful day.'

'How was your day?'

She had told him she had plans Friday, so ignored his messages. She thought about what a contradiction he was. How had any woman in her right mind mistreated that man? He was just vulnerable enough for her to win over without him knowing he was being played.

She was certain the other women were not smart in their pursuit of him. She would let him pursue her, and she knew that it would help that she had a date with Drew on Saturday night. Drew had earned a greater immediate use. Not only was he still a candidate to be her provider, he was also number one as a distraction since Lawrence was a growing interest. The children were inconsequential.

32 DELORES – SATURDAY

At 8:45 am there was a message from Lawrence.

'Hello beautiful. I miss you :)'

It was perfect timing. Her meeting began at 9 and the message put a great smile on her face.

'I'm counting down the hours until I get on the plane'

'Dinner at 7 at Tabu Grill?'

'Perfect.'

'Big hug and kiss. I'm so grateful you came into my life'

After her meeting with Dolly, Delores was driven to the Learjet. Today she decided to have Chee-yong prepare the jet's queen bed for her so she could lie down for a portion of the flight. She wanted to be fresh and awake for dinner with Lawrence. Her nap instead lasted the entire flight. When she landed there was a message from Lawrence.

'I hope you're not too tired for dinner.'

'No. I had a long nap on the flight.'

For the first time he did not respond instantly.

'Good. I just got up from a wonderful nap, too :) I miss you.'

'I miss you, too. See you at 7 at Tabu.'

'Big hug and kiss :)'

33 MAIZIE – SATURDAY

Maizie slept in until nearly 8 am on Saturday, and enjoyed a leisurely breakfast. With plans to meet Lawrence again she felt like she had arrived in a life full of new possibilities. The plan was going to work. She would have it all very soon. It would be so much better with the handsome one than with sweaty Drew.

She decided to open the old site and see if she had any more messages from Lawrence. She smiled when she saw she had guessed correctly. She thought he would be nervous about being stood up and send another message. In fact, there were two.

'Good night. I can't wait to see you in the morning.'

She had received that at 9:15 pm Friday. This morning at 6:40 he had written also.

'Good morning. I'll see you in just a few hours. I thought we could walk along the beach with our coffee. Text me if anything changes: 949-555-2345'

She decided not to write back. She wanted him to sweat it. She also wanted him to trust that she was a woman of her word. Maizie realized Lawrence would have seen that she had been active both days, and not have responded. With the timing of his messages, he would be able to deduce when she had gone online.

He probably assumed that she had been out with another match. Perfect. He knew there was competition.

Maizie wore the same outfit she had worn when she first ran into Jared at the music festival. Not only was it a comfortable outfit, but also she looked even better in it now that her skin was sun-kissed from the summer.

The corner cafe was a quick two minute walk down a flight of stairs and less than half a mile away once she reached the bottom. Lawrence was waiting for her at the counter as he had said he would. He looked peaceful in his worn jeans and white t-shirt. He was wearing sandals, and his face was not shaven. Though she did not care for the scruffy look on most men, it made him look even more comfortable and even slightly vulnerable. It was so easy to be in his company, and even easier to feel in control of him.

She took a moment to just drink in his presence. She wanted to stay in control. He was strangely more intoxicating than he had been a couple nights ago. He was radiating sex appeal, and it was not something he appeared to exert any effort in doing.

"Good morning!" she greeted him.

He turned to see her and a giant smile spread across his face.

"Hi, Maizie."

Lawrence still seemed somehow nervous, like it would take him a little while to fully recover from his fear of being stood up. His ex-wife clearly had mistreated this gentle man.

"You look beautiful. I thought we could get a coffee and take it to go. It would be nice to walk along the water. Are you up for that?"

"Yes. I would like that."

"What do you want to drink? I'll go get it."

"I'll have a tall house blend. Black."

"That's what I get. Well, actually I put in a couple drops of half and half."

He was shy about that. She liked that he was putting their actions together, making them similar so she would seem more familiar to him.

He returned with their drinks, and they crossed the coast highway to the beach. They walked along drinking their coffee and talking. He pointed out a few places of interest, including the balcony where they had first met for drinks. It looked different during the day. Finally, they arrived at a point at which they could go no further without scaling a rough set of rocks, where they definitely would either get scraped on the rocks or drenched by a wave.

"This is called Lover's Beach," he said. "Hey, how long have we been holding hands? How did that happen?"

She smiled. "I didn't realize that either."

"This is like fate. I feel like I have known you forever. It is just so easy to be around you."

She chuckled. "Yes, it is unreal that we just met a couple days ago."

She felt uneasy about what he had just said because she knew that was a warning from the site's disclaimer. She decided to play along with what he said. Everything else indicated he was falling for her fast. All men did. She was certain she was totally in control, again taking in the power of the ocean. Every time a wave crashed onto the sand she thought of the power she had over this man.

He suddenly seemed extremely nervous again. He pulled her closer to him and put an arm around her back. She was certain he was going to kiss her, and she knew it would be more than the light kisses the other night. He wanted a real kiss. She decided to make it difficult for him. What fun would it be otherwise?

"I need to throw away my cup," she said and walked to a trashcan that was positioned next to a nearby flight of cement stairs that provided beach access from the road above.

He looked after her like a lost puppy dog as she made her trip to the trash can and back. When she was a couple feet away, he reached out and pulled her to him. He kissed her gently at first, and then deeper with passion.

He pulled back and said, "I could kiss your lips all day. You are amazing. My opinion of the site has just gone up several notches."

She laughed and responded with a light kiss instead of words. She wanted to play along, and she did not want to waste words when he would remember her lips more than anything she could say.

"If this wasn't already named Lover's Beach, then I'd call it that anyway after being here with you."

Maizie was beginning to sense that he was acting more interested in her than he really was. Maybe he was just nervous.

He pulled her close and kissed her again. She ignored her doubt and returned the kiss.

He led her over to a small inlet in the nearby cliff, where they were obstructed from the view of others.

His contradiction was evident again. His actions were those of a man who had done this many times, yet his manner was truly nervous and he seemed honestly interested in her. Maybe he had read about how to seduce a lady in a men's magazine and never had the opportunity to attempt it. She decided to enjoy the kissing and continued to ignore the moments of doubt.

"I live just at the top of these stairs. Would you like me to go get a couple towels for us so we can relax on the beach for a while? I would invite you up, but that just seems a little forward. You can wait here."

"Actually, I'd love to see where you live."

"I don't trust myself not to throw myself at you if I took you to my house."

"You don't have to worry. I can fend for myself."

She winked at him. He seemed to be the most nervous he had been that morning. This certainly was new to him. He did not know what to do. She would guide him gently.

"Let's go, then."

He led her up the stairs and then up a small hill toward his house.

"Do you like wood?"

"That's an odd question."

"My house has a lot of wood. Do you like wood floors and furniture?"

"Oh. Yes. I love anything solid."

She was now even more intrigued to see his house. It would be her first time inside a Laguna Beach house that could give her a taste of the lifestyle her future held. That was what she wanted to see.

His house was hidden from view of the street by a stucco garage with steel door, and framed with minimal yet flawless landscaping. He led her down the path that ran along the garage, onto the deck that overlooked the ocean, and through double glass doors into a large master suite with an expansive view of the coastline. The ceiling had slats of whitewashed wood with whitewashed wood beams running perpendicular. The floor was also wood, and a king size bed was framed in a substantial gunmetal headboard and footboard. There was only a sheet on the bed.

"Sorry. I wasn't expecting company. My comforter is in the wash. Oh, here, have a seat."

He picked up a set of pillows from the nearby sofa and put them back on the bed so there was a place for Maizie to sit.

"That's okay. I'm all full of sand. I don't want to make a mess of your house."

"Don't worry about it. Well, this is the master bedroom. Obviously. Um..."

He was nervous again.

"Your house is very nice. I see why you asked about wood."

He laughed a little nervously.

"I'll show you around a bit. Didn't you say you liked Jimi Hendrix? Look. I have this full set of Jimi Hendrix records. They are in perfect condition."

This was endearing. He was like a child showing off to her. She didn't believe that he truly liked Jimi Hendrix, though. She walked over and began sorting through the records. It was a full collection.

"Wow, that is amazing. Do you have a record player?"

"In the living room."

They found themselves standing inches apart.

"I think you're too far from me right now. I want you closer," he whispered.

He pulled her close and kissed her again. They kissed a few minutes and then tumbled onto his bed.

"How did I get so lucky?" he asked. "You are beautiful, smart, and fun. It is so easy to be with you. I can't believe it's only been two days."

She didn't believe that he was being entirely sincere.

"Actually, we've only spent four hours together."

"Happy four hours, then. They have been. I am so grateful you came into my life."

True to his word he was all over her, kissing her and touching her body hungrily now that they were in the privacy of his home. She could feel that he was aroused. She pressed her body closer to his and then, true to her word, rolled far away from him.

"I have to put on the brakes."

"Okay," he said. "Let's talk. Talking is good. I just want to be with you."

She giggled. They talked for a little while about silly pranks they had pulled in college, and it was fun. It seemed like she had known him forever, and she was able to gain a sense of his genuine, yet nervous nature. It must be his nervousness that made her doubt his sincerity earlier.

"Oh, you said you like to ski except for the part about getting cold. And you're the one from the East Coast."

He got up from the bed and went to his dresser.

"Look, I have these great long underwear. They're made of some material that keeps you warm when it is cold and cool when you start to build up a sweat. It's amazing technology. I don't know how the fibers of the material can be so smart. Have you ever heard of these?"

He held out the top with the label turned to her.

"No, I've never heard of those. I can't believe you're showing me your underwear, silly."

Again he was showing off like a schoolboy, and she had the impression that he may have bought those just to show her. It seemed rehearsed.

"I just thought you should know about them since you'd be interested in getting some. I don't want you to be cold."

He returned to the bed and pulled her close again.

"May I?"

Instead of saying yes, she rolled over on top of him and leaned down to kiss him.

"You're amazing, Maizie. I just want to kiss you all day. Is that okay with you?"

Again she didn't speak. She kissed him tentatively.

"I'm so glad you came into my life. I really like you, Maizie."

She doubted his sincerity. She did not know who he was. Something was strange about the entire morning. She did not want to think about it. She did not want to know.

She decided to just not care and go with it. She would pretend that they truly were brought together by fate, as he had said several times, and see if she felt anything as it all unfolded. She wanted to know what it would be like and didn't care how it would turn out.

"I like you, too, Lawrence."

She leaned down and kissed him again. This time she did not hold back. She had nothing to lose.

He kissed her, ran his hands over her body, and worked her shirt off slowly.

She rolled off of him and pulled him on top of her. She pulled his shirt off over his head and continued to kiss him. She forgot who he was. She didn't know anyway.

He was able to get his pants off and she could feel him pressing against her leg. Their kisses were getting hungrier. Before she could think about it her shorts were off and had been flung across the room.

Their kisses slowed. He was tentative. She was curious. He pulled away from her and spread her legs apart, holding them down. He moved closer very slowly on his knees, and looked down at her. His eyes were dancing. He wasn't smiling. She wasn't smiling either.

She grinned. He leaned in to kiss her neck.

She leaned her head back and let herself enjoy his lips on her for a moment before she mimicked his move by kissing his neck. He chuckled.

She pulled back and they looked at each other. Neither of them was smiling.

He didn't believe her. She didn't believe him.

The game was up.

She didn't care. She gave him a mischievous grin as if to dare him to make another move. He grinned and took the dare. He was inside her.

With nothing to prove and no need to continue a game, they spent the day alternating between sex and napping. They each left the bed a couple times to use the bathroom. They didn't speak.

At 5:30 he motioned toward the door and said, "You have to go now. I have plans."

"Are you at least going to walk me out?"

"Are you fucking kidding me?"

"You don't have to be such a jerk about it!"

"The door is right there."

He picked up his phone and ignored her entirely. She thought about shattering his record collection, but she knew he didn't listen to Jimi Hendrix. She thought about throwing the records at him, but she knew he would just laugh at her.

She was powerless. She couldn't believe it. She stood frozen in the middle of his bedroom. He hadn't even shown her the rest of his house. She was angry, and at the same time she was completely at peace. It felt good.

"Get dressed and I'll walk you out."

She did.

He did.

No farewells were necessary.

Maizie walked home alone along the same path she had walked with Lawrence that morning. When she got home, she was not surprised to see that Lawrence had deleted her as a match on the service. They would no longer see each other's activity.

Who was he anyway?

She got ready for her date with Drew. She smirked as she looked in the mirror. She knew she could trust her intuition. This match she knew she controlled.

34 LAWRENCE – SATURDAY

Lawrence was smug as he headed into the dining room to meet Delores. He was the picture of success. He sure had proven his masculinity in bed that day. He was a master. He liked that he could devour girls like Maizie. He knew she liked it, too. And if she didn't, that was her problem.

He smiled. He was so good at this.

And Delores. He had played his cards so perfectly with the woman. She was beautiful, naïve, and she just happened to be worth hundreds of millions of dollars. He had done his research.

He was going to make sure to get in on her fortune. He was sick of working. He was sick of providing.

Delores would be too happy to let him in.

How had he gotten so lucky?

He was just that good.

ABOUT THE AUTHOR

Heidi Pine has been writing short stories since 1983. Her first published story was written at a young authors' workshop in Milwaukee, Wisconsin, when she was in sixth grade. At age 13 she wrote a regular column in a weekly newspaper. When she is not working as an engineer or technical writer, Heidi enjoys traveling, cooking, reading, and open water swimming. She lives in Laguna Beach.